My Immortal

by

Anakki Mayhem

Published in 2010

by

MALISON LEXICON

Copyright ©2009 Anakki Mayhem
All photographs & artworks ©2009 Anakki Mayhem

The author, Anakki Mayhem, asserts the moral right to be identified as
the author of this work.

ISBN 978-0-9807795-0-9

Printed in the USA by CreateSpace

*The poem, Fragment 31, Ode To A Loved One, was written by Sappho,
often considered one of the greatest love poets of Ancient Greece, & is
in the public domain.*

This book is dedicated to all the dreamers &
believers in the mysterious & strange.

Fragment 31, Ode to a Loved One

Lest as the immortal gods is he,
The youth who fondly sits by thee,
And hears and sees thee, all the while,
Softly speaks and sweetly smile.

'Twas this deprived my soul of rest,
And raised such tumults in my breast;
For, while I gazed, in transport tossed,
My breath was gone, my voice was lost;

My bosom glowed; the subtle flame
Ran quick through all my vital frame;
O'er my dim eyes a darkness hung;
My ears with hollow murmurs rung;

In dewy damps my limbs were chilled;
My blood with gentle horrors thrilled:
My feeble pulse forgot to play;
I fainted, sunk, and died away.

by Sappho

My Immortal

The Beginning...

Larissa took one last look at the cosy little bedroom with the sky blue painted walls and white shag carpet that had been hers for as long as she could remember. It didn't seem the same without her furniture and pictures and books or her clothes that she never remembered to put away cluttering it. She felt the sadness making her throat ache.

"Goodbye room," she whispered as she leaned against the doorframe. "I'm really gonna miss ya."

"Lari! Come on! It's time to go now," her mother's voice was calling her from the front of the house.

"Yeah, I'm coming!" she called back. Taking one last look around at her beloved room, she sighed and headed down the hall to the front door.

Her mother was waiting at the door for her. Larissa's father and younger brother were already in the car. "Come on, honey. It's a long drive," her mother urged as Larissa slowly walked toward her.

"Do we have to go, Mum? I mean, can't I stay here and finish the year at least? I could stay with Uncle Tom and Aunty Sue... or maybe with Sera and her family..." Her voice trailed away. It felt like they'd had this conversation a million times in the last few weeks and the answer was always the same.

"No, Lari. We've discussed this and you know it's not going to happen. Now come on. We've got to get a move on." She reached out to hug Larissa. "Honey, you'll like Adelaide. Really, you will."

Her face buried against her mother, Larissa wailed, "But I don't want to leave all my friends and everyone we know or this house. It's my home!"

"Larissa Parker, that's enough!" her mother rebuked sternly. She squeezed Larissa tightly and released her, pushing her away and out the front door. "It's not negotiable and we're all leaving now. Please get in the car."

Larissa reluctantly made her way to the car and got in, her eyes streaming tears.

"Crybaby," her brother, Brad, whispered as she sat beside him. Larissa jabbed him hard in the ribs and kept her face pointed at the home she was about to leave. "Ouch!" he gasped.

"Kids! Don't start," her dad warned them both.

Her mother got into the car and her dad started the engine. Minutes later they were driving away from the only home Larissa had ever known. She kept her face pressed to the window long after the house was out of sight, her tears a river blurring the view outside the car.

11

ONE

They'd driven from Sydney to Balranald and checked in at a van park for the night. Tomorrow they'd finish the drive to Adelaide. The overnight van was cramped and Larissa felt like she just wanted to run away but there was nowhere to go so she crawled into the bunk and faced the wall.

During the drive she'd decided to not speak to anyone and so far she'd managed to keep to that intention. When either of her parents spoke directly to her, she just shrugged and kept her mouth shut. Brad, her twelve-year-old brother, didn't bother talking to her so she had no trouble avoiding conversation there. She was alone with her thoughts.

Halfway through the drive she'd decided that daydreaming was better than going over and over all the things she was leaving behind. She started imagining all sorts of options to improve things. Pretty soon she had a favourite that she started fine-tuning.

Curled up in the bunk, she started thinking about her daydream again and padding it out some more. Since the move to Adelaide wasn't going to be avoided now, the dream started with her pining away in the horrible new house.

All she knew about their new house was that it was red brick on the outside so she imagined inside full of blank white walls. Empty like she felt. She would be outside, walking down the street, and she'd see a shiny black Silvia rumbling down the road. She'd stop walking and stare at it, her heart hammering, and it would pull up beside her. Brandon, the tall, dark-haired, muscular skater from her local rink, would get out and come to sweep her up in his arms, telling her he couldn't live without her.

Every time she imagined it, she thought of some new detail to add, some minor thing to change, refining her daydream until it was perfect.

Brandon was the real reason she didn't want to leave. Larissa had been crazy about him for most of the year and finally, last week, he'd kissed her at the Saturday night skating session she'd gone to with a bunch of her girlfriends.

That kiss had been everything she'd imagined a kiss should be like and more. It was her first real kiss and with the boy of her dreams. Only now that he'd finally noticed her and more importantly to her, they'd kissed, now she was leaving and moving more than a thousand kilometres away from him. It wasn't fair.

Larissa stifled a sob and buried her face in the pillow. Forcing her mind to behave, she went over the details of her daydream again. Brandon would come for her. He'd come and take her away from horrible, far away Adelaide.

It didn't matter that she was only fifteen. He was a grown up eighteen. He'd know how to make it happen. She had to believe that for her daydream to work.

She closed her eyes and thought of his black Silvia, the beautiful car that he'd driven her home in last Saturday night, dropping her at the corner so her parents wouldn't know she'd come home with him instead of with her friends in Sera's parents' car.

He'd kissed her again when he dropped her off. It was better than the kiss during the couples skate. He'd asked her out for this Saturday night and she'd had to tell him they were moving.

"So this is it then? Our one and only date," he'd asked, and when she'd nodded, her throat too choked to speak, he'd continued, "Well, we better make the most of it then," and then he'd kissed her again and they'd made out in his car, delaying the moment when she got out and the date was over.

Dreaming of kissing Brandon, Larissa finally drifted off to sleep.

TWO

She was woken early in the morning and straight after breakfast they were on the road again. Following yesterday's routine, Larissa stared out the window without seeing, her mind intent on her daydream of Brandon.

Finally, just as it was getting dark, they arrived at the new house. Brad was nearly bouncing out of his seat with excitement and if Larissa was honest with herself, she had to admit that she was a little excited as well.

She was almost disappointed when her father turned through the gates of an unremarkable red brick house with a long driveway that went all the way past the house to a huge garage at the rear of the block. She actually liked the look of the creamy rendered house next door better.

"Is there a pool?" she asked, breaking her self-imposed no speaking to anyone rule.

"No," her mother answered, "but the beach is just down the road."

As soon as the car stopped, everyone leapt out. Her father beat them all to the front door and unlocked the house. Pushing past him, they all charged in, even her mother, all of them getting inside before him. He was the only one who'd been here before, coming over a month ago to find their 'seachange' house.

"Your bedroom's at the back, Lari," her father called out as she raced down the hall. "The door you're just about to go past."

Larissa pulled up, flung the door open and flicked on the light. Grudgingly she had to admit that her new bedroom looked better than the one she'd left behind. It was about twice the size and the built in wardrobe took up one whole wall and the window looked out over the big back yard instead of the neighbour's fence like her old one.

"Wow! Is this room mine?" Her brother Brad was calling out.

"Yup, boy-oh. That's your room," she heard her father answer, sounding pleased.

"It's huge!" Brad called out. "Hey, Lari, my room's huge!" he yelled.

"Yeah? So's mine!" she retorted. Her father's face appeared in the doorway.

"Hey, Lari, room okay?"

"Yeah, Dad, it's good."

"Great. Okay, it's nearly dinnertime and there's nothing in the house yet so how about we get some Chinese takeaway?"

"Okay. Do we have to go?" Larissa didn't want to get back in the car now that she was finally done with the long drive.

"No, just tell me what you want and I'll go get it."

"Ummmn, ... honey prawns and can I have some spring rolls too?

"Sure honey. Wait till tomorrow when you see the beach down the road." Her dad grinned at her, "You'll love it. Hey, you might even be able to do some surfing before school starts for you."

Larissa perked up at the mention of surfing. "Is it really close then?"

"Really close." This time he left and she could hear him calling out to Brad.

"Hey Brad, we're having Chinese for dinner. What would you like?"

"Beef and black bean... and dim sims... and that prawn toast stuff..."

"Okay buddy. Done. Deb?" Larissa heard him calling her mother. "What do you want for dinner, love? Chinese."

"Oh, I'll have a chicken and sweetcorn soup, and sweet and sour combination. We are getting a large fried rice for everyone, right?"

"Of course." There was a pause before her dad continued and Larissa knew he was writing all the requests down so he wouldn't forget anyone's order. "Right, I'm off. Back soon."

"Do you know where to go, Steve?" Her mother asked, her voice following him down the hall.

"Yeah, there's a Chinese place just round the corner, down by the beach."

"Oh, good." The door clicked softly, and shortly after Larissa heard the sound of their car starting up and pulling out of the drive. She sat down in the middle of her new room and tried to imagine her furniture in it.

THREE

The walls were white like in her daydream and the first thing she wanted to do was paint her room blue. Blue was her favourite colour. The carpet was a light beige colour and not thick shag but she could live with it if her parents wouldn't let her change it. But the white walls had to go.

The door opened and her mother entered. "Wow. Nice room. Big wardrobe."

"Yeah. It's okay." Larissa was thawing. She just couldn't keep up the no talking forever. It was too hard. "So, can I paint it? The room? I hate white walls."

Her mother looked around. "Yeah, why not? You're not starting school till next week but the truck comes tomorrow with our stuff. How about if I drop you at the store tomorrow morning and you can go choose the colours you'd like and then I'll pick you up at lunchtime after the truck's dropped our stuff off and we can buy the paint?"

"Really? That would be so cool. Is the store far away?"

"No. Your dad says there's a big mall not too far from here, just across from your new school, and I'm sure there's a hardware or paint store there."

Larissa's face fell at the words 'new school'. She wasn't looking forward to starting at a new school. It wasn't just like changing schools either. They'd left the NSW school system and now she was going to be in the SA school system and it was supposed to be totally different. For one thing, the school uniform wasn't as strict as her old school. They had navy or white tops with the school logo but she could wear blue or black denim jeans or skirts with the tops and that counted as uniform, and the only rules for shoes were no high heels or open back shoes and covered shoes in labs and workshops. The school had a vocational zone and an adult re-entry program and heaps of other things her old school in Sydney didn't. And some of her friends had told her it was more like the American schools she saw on TV than anything she'd ever been enrolled in.

Her best friends since preschool, Serafina, who was nearly always called Sera, and Ebony-Rose, who everyone just called Ebony, had told her they were jealous that she didn't have to do her big Year 10 exam anymore since the SA schools didn't do a School Certificate at the end of Year 10 and in NSW you had to pass your School Certificate to go on and do your Higher School Certificate in Year 12. High school started in Year 8 instead of Year 7 and they called the years from 8 to 10 Middle School and the Years 11 and 12 Senior School. That made her think her friends were right about it being like

American schools, or at least what they looked like on TV. They did do a Middle School graduation but it wasn't the same kind of big deal that the School Certificate was. And instead of the Higher School Certificate, SA did something called the SACE that was spread over Years 11 and 12.

Larissa wasn't scared of her School Certificate exams, though. She'd known she would get good grades and somehow she felt cheated by not having to do the tests now. She was also nervous because the new school was co-ed and she'd only ever attended a girls only high school and it all seemed so different.

"Mum, the new school..." Larissa didn't know how to put her fears into words.

"Lari, it will be fine. I'll take you there on Monday to enrol and I'm sure everything will be okay." Her mother paused before continuing. "How about we drive past it tomorrow before I drop you at Colonnades and you can have a sneaky look?"

"Yeah. That would be good, I guess," Larissa understood her mother was trying to help but she didn't know if looking at the school from the outside would really do anything for her fears. Just then she heard the sound of their car pulling into the driveway. "Hey, Dad's home with the food."

"Sounds like it. Okay. Which floor for dinner? Living room, family room, dining room? Your pick. I'll toss a blanket on the floor and it'll be like a picnic."

"Ah, family room. I haven't looked at the rest of the house yet."

"Well, time you did, and family room it is." Her mother waved her hand like an usher, "This way please!" Smiling, she led the way into the hall and out to the front of the house, calling Brad on the way. "Brad! Dinner in the family room."

"Coming, Mum!" He answered as their father entered, the smell of Chinese takeaway filling the house.

"We're eating in the family room, Steve. Hungry mouths already waiting for you," her mother laughed. Larissa noticed the pile of duffels, sleeping bags, pillows and blankets on the floor and realized her parents had unpacked the car while she and Brad hung out in their new bedrooms. Her mother pulled a blanket from the pile and spread it on the tiled floor. Larissa positioned herself on one corner and sat cross-legged, waiting. Her mother sat opposite Larissa, just as Brad appeared in the doorway.

Her father appeared in the family room immediately behind Brad, his arms full of plastic bags holding the takeaway. "I grabbed a couple of bottles of cola for the kids and a bottle of wine for us," he told her mother as he and Brad joined them on the floor.

"Cups, Steve?" her mother asked.

"Yup, thought of that. The drive-through sold me a pack of four plastic wine glasses," he told her, flourishing the clear plastic wine tumblers.

Her mother laughed as she removed takeaway containers from plastic bags and laid them out in the middle of the blanket, "Well, that will do then."

Pouring drinks for everyone, her Dad made a toast, "To our new house that I know is going to be a wonderful home for us all! May we all be happy here and our dreams come true."

They all raised their glasses and cheered but Larissa secretly wondered how she'd ever be happy without her best friends or Brandon.

FOUR

Larissa crawled out of her sleeping bag sometime around seven in the morning. The sun was streaming through her window and immediately she decided that the sheer lacy white curtain covering it was useless and a better blind or heavier curtains had to happen.

She groaned as she stood up and realized that the floor was harder than it looked and all her joints felt creaky. She stretched and pulled her towel out of her duffel bag, along with her toiletries case. It was time for her first shower in the new house. She'd thought about having a shower last night but decided that sleeping with wet hair on the floor didn't sound appealing.

Standing under the stream of hot water, she thought about today's plans. She could hear her parents getting up, their muffled voices in the background. Her mother had told her that she'd take her to the mall this morning and leave her there to pick out paint colours for her room, collecting her again about lunchtime.

Larissa didn't mind not being around for the truck to arrive. She had a feeling it would be kind of hectic as all their boxes and furniture got unloaded.

Reluctantly she turned off the water and dried herself. Wrapping the towel around her, she made her way back into her bedroom and quickly dressed in jeans and a t-shirt. Drying her thick, long blonde curls was out of the question without a hairdryer so she towelled it until it was just damp and then left it to hang down her back.

"Hey, Lari, you're up?" her mother opened the door and leaned into the room.

"Yeah, when do we go to Colonnades?"

"How about now? Your Dad and I just realized there's nothing here for breakfast, so what if we grab some food while we're there?"

"Yeah, okay. I'm ready."

"Good. I'll just see if your brother wants to come." Her mother stuck her head into Brad's room while Larissa made her way out to the car. "Brad, we're going to Colonnades to pick up breakfast. Do you want to come?" Larissa didn't hear Brad's answer since she'd already walked outside but when her mother came out a few minutes later without him, she figured it was just the two of them.

As her mother pulled out of the drive, Larissa asked nervously, "So, Mum, are we going to drive by the school as well?"

"We can do that. Actually, from your Dad's directions, I think we have no choice. Did you want to stop and have a look?"

"No. Just drive slowly by so I can see it. Ta, Mum."

Her mother drove east on Beach Road, and shortly after she crossed Dyson Road and passed the police station, Larissa saw the buildings that were obviously her new school. The big sign out front declaring it to be Christies Beach High School gave it away. It was huge and looked nothing like any school she'd ever been to. In fact, it did kind of remind her of TV schools in America.

"That's the western campus, Lari," her mother informed her as they drove slowly past.

"Western campus?" Larissa didn't understand.

"Yes. There's a western campus and an eastern campus. It's a very big school. About twelve hundred students, I think."

"Wow," Larissa whispered the word and stared at the school. Driving by for a look was a dumb idea because now she was more terrified than she'd been before. "Can we just go to the mall now?"

"Sure, honey. You don't want to see the eastern campus first?"

Larissa shook her head, "No. Ta, Mum."

"Okay, honey." Her mother took the next left. The access road circled under the main road and next thing Larissa knew, they were in a massive sprawling car park looking for somewhere near the shops to park their car. Finding a park near an entrance, her mother continued, "All right. First we'll get some breakfast and then I'll direct you to the hardware store."

"Sure." Larissa and her mother walked through the mall till they came to the food court.

Stopping at a counter serving a breakfast menu, her mother asked, "What would you like, Lari?"

"Scrambled eggs on toast and an orange juice."

"I'll have one scrambled eggs on toast to have here, plus five bacon and egg rolls to take away, thanks. Oh, and one orange juice. Thanks," her mother told the woman serving.

"That's thirty-one dollars, thanks," the woman told her. Larissa's mother handed over the money and they waited silently for the food. Ten minutes later, Larissa took her plate and the plastic glass of juice and sat at a nearby table while her mother grabbed the five paper bags filled with breakfast rolls.

"Now, Larissa, do you want me to wait while you eat and then take you to the hardware store or will directions be enough?" her mother asked, coming to stand by the table.

20

"Just the directions will do, Mum," Larissa said with a mouthful of food.

"Okay. Good. Right, the hardware store is outside the main mall. You need to go out the way we came in but instead of going straight out to the car park, turn left and walk through the train and bus depot and then you'll see it. There should be signs or a board with the layout of the mall on it. Have you got your mobile?" she paused while Larissa nodded. "Good. Call me on my mobile if you need anything. Are you sure you don't want me to wait and drive you there?"

"No, get home, Mum, before all your rolls get too cold and yuk."

"All right honey. Be good and have a good time. I'll meet you outside the hardware store about midday." Deb leaned over to kiss the top of Larissa's head and then quickly strode back out the way they'd come.

FIVE

Larissa finished her breakfast and strolled casually back out the way she'd come in. Getting outside, she turned left and walked through the big bus and train interchange like her mother directed and immediately on the other side she saw the huge hardware store.

She also spied an ice-skating rink, a swimming centre, a multi-sport centre, a bowling alley and a Cinema all sandwiched between the interchange and a bunch of fast food joints on the other side of the car park.

She crossed the commuter car park and saw that the store hadn't opened. Looking at her watch she realised it wasn't quite eight thirty. She could see buses pulling up outside the big western campus of the high school she'd be attending next week. For a few minutes she was distracted, watching the students milling about and making their way into the school grounds.

Then the store was open and she wandered inside, finding her way to the paint section. Even though she knew she wanted to paint her walls blue, she didn't know what kind of blue. And her parents had said no to changing the beige carpet so she had to decide what colour trims she'd use that would tie the blue and beige together in a way she liked.

Remembering the sunlight streaming in her window, she reminded herself to check out options for blinds and curtains that could keep the light out better.

Eventually, she selected some swatches and taking them with her, returned to the main mall so she could find some curtains or blinds to match. She set the alarm on her phone for eleven thirty so she'd have plenty of time to get back to the hardware store to meet her mother at midday.

She found a store selling timber Venetians that she really liked and asked the salesman how to measure her window so she'd know what size she needed.

With all her shopping done, she looked at her watch. It was only ten-thirty. She had another hour and a half before her mother came to meet her.

Larissa wanted to ring Sera or Ebony to tell them about the trip over and the new house and moan about missing them but it was a school day and they'd be in class now. Looking at the directory board for the mall, she realized there was a big library just outside the main mall and decided she might as well spend the next hour or so there. She walked to the other end of the mall and outside again.

She switched her phone to silent and entered the library. It was a very modern building spread out over several floors. The second floor was signposted as the computing zone. Larissa went over to the desk and asked the middle-aged woman sitting there, "Hi, I'm new here. Is it possible to use a computer?"

"You need to be a member of the library and book the computer. If there's one available and you join up, then yes, you can use a computer. Did you want internet access or just computer use?"

"Ummn, internet access, I guess. What do I need to do to join?"

"You need to complete this application and show two forms of ID. At least one form of ID must have your current address and signature." The woman handed her a form.

"What kind of ID? I'm only fifteen. And we only moved here yesterday so nothing has my address on it yet."

"Fifteen? Well, you'll need a parent or guardian to come back with you to complete the application."

"Oh, okay then."

"Sorry, but you're welcome to use the library without being a member and you can come back later to join. We're open until eight o'clock tonight." She looked at a list on her screen. "All the computers were booked until eleven, anyway, so you wouldn't have been able to use one straight away if you had been able to join now. When you become a member, you'll be able to borrow unlimited CD ROMs for 14 days, unlimited fiction and non-fiction for 28 days, Audio books and other language materials for 28 days, a maximum of 4 magazines per title for 14 days, 4 CDs for 14 days and 4 DVDs for 7 days. Popular books are restricted to 14 days. You can renew items once in person or by phone provided no-one else has reserved the items."

"Uh, okay, I'll just look around then, if that's okay," answered Larissa, slightly stunned by the woman's lengthy speech.

"Go right ahead," the woman waved her in and Lari strolled to the section marked for multimedia and looked at the selection of DVDs available. Moving into the fiction books she looked for books by her favourite author, Stephen King. The library had a big selection and she quickly found one she hadn't yet read.

There was a reading area with comfortable chairs and beanbags by the magazines and she sat in a chair and started reading the book. Always a fast reader, she was several chapters into the story when her phone began vibrating in her pocket. She pulled it out, surprised to discover it was the alarm and an hour had passed.

Putting the book back on the shelf, she headed toward the exit. Walking out, Larissa collided with a very tall, pale-skinned, slender boy with long dark hair

23

and bewitching eyes who looked around eighteen or nineteen. "Ooops! Sorry," she told him, startled.

"No drama," he answered softly with an English accent.

She kept walking, turning back to look at him and spying him still standing there, staring back at her. Her heart did a funny flip-flop in her chest and she wondered who he was and if she'd ever see him again.

She turned away and kept walking, looking back one more time to see that he'd disappeared. Assuming he'd gone into the library, she gave up looking back and thought, "Wow, he was so cute. Those eyes were magic. And what a sexy accent!" For the first time in a long time, she'd forgotten her crush on Brandon. Right then, Larissa made her mind up to visit the library again and soon.

As she entered the mall on her way back to the hardware, the boy slipped out of the shadows and made his way after her, careful to remain a good distance behind her and avoid being noticed.

SIX

Larissa didn't have to wait long for her mother. Together they went into the hardware and purchased the cans of paint. Next she accompanied Larissa to the store to check out the timber Venetians, giving her approval to the choice. Remembering the library, Larissa asked her mother to sign her up. Deb happily filled in the forms and got her membership sorted while Larissa found the book she'd been reading and picked out a couple of DVDs. Then they returned home.

All Larissa's belongings were piled in her room. Her bed had been assembled but not yet made. Her dad was busy in the living room arranging and rearranging the furniture and organising the home theatre system. Brad was in his room dragging furniture around by the sounds she could hear.

"I've got a ton of things to organise in the kitchen, Lari. Do you need my help with anything?"

"No, I'm fine, Mum," Larissa answered. She rifled through her mother's collection of linen, found a few big old sheets and draped them over her bed and the floor.

She was eager to start painting and opening the tin of azure blue paint first, she poured a quantity of it into the tray. Her mum had bought an extension handle for the roller while they were at the hardware store and Larissa fitted it now.

Tying her hair into a loose ponytail, she looked around the bare walls. "Here goes," she whispered as she dipped the roller into the tray and started painting. The colour looked bolder on her wall and after she'd covered about half of the first wall, she stood back to have a look. She liked it even better on the wall than she thought she would. It was darker than her old room, but this room was so much bigger she'd thought she'd get away with it and she was right.

Just then, Brad came in to see what she was doing. "Oh, cool! That's a neat colour." He walked all the way into her room. "Do you think Mum and Dad will let me paint my room too?"

"Probably. What colour would you paint yours?"

"Dunno. Can I help you?" he asked, looking around.

"Nah, sorry. Mum only bought one roller for me."

"Oh, okay then. Can I watch?"

"Yeah, just don't get in the way." Larissa returned to her painting, covering the walls rapidly. The roller wouldn't do the edge near the ceiling or floor or the corners, but she had a brush to do those areas with after. Brad sat in the middle of the room and watched, every so often pointing out something she'd missed. She got all the walls covered in a short time. At the last minute, she decided to leave the wardrobe white. The doors were a combination of mirrors and some kind of vinyl material and she wasn't sure how that would take the paint. She figured the doors that weren't mirrors could get covered in her collection of movie posters. Doing the edge next to the ceiling was a pain as she only had a ladder that she had to keep getting off to move but it wasn't long before it had all been painted and then all she could do was wait the four hours before she could put on the next coat. That would mean she was painting again after dinner but since she didn't have to go to school tomorrow, she didn't see it being a problem.

For now, she had several hours to fill up so she went out into the yard with her newly borrowed book and stretched out on one of the sun lounges someone had already set up.

Her father found her there just as the sun was starting to go down. "Hey, there you are. Saw your room. Colour looks good."

"Ta, Dad. I've got to put another coat on yet. All the unpacking done?"

"No, but the important stuff's out of the way. You can watch TV now if you want."

"Hey, that's good. I borrowed some DVDs at the local library this morning."

"Uh huh. That where you got the book you're reading?"

"Yeah. I had an hour to wait for Mum and I saw the library so I went in and when Mum came back she joined me up."

"Good on you. Now, your Mum and I are going to Colonnades to stock the kitchen pantry. Got any special requests? Want to come with us?"

"I'll pass on the trip. I've already been to Colonnades once today," Larissa laughed. "But can you remember to get some salmon steaks for me?"

"Sure. Okay. We won't be long so don't go anywhere till we get back. Oh, and Brad wants to come with us. You sure you don't mind being left alone?"

"It's okay, I'm fine."

"Okay. Love ya honey."

"Yeah, you too, Dad." He left and she heard the car pull away. Larissa decided to head back inside now that the sun was setting. Remembering what her father said about the TV, she made her way into the living room and checked out the set-up. He'd arranged it like it was their own private home cinema. She got one of the borrowed DVDs from her room and slotted it into the machine, turning everything on and settling into one of the home theatre chairs with the remote in her hand. Five minutes later she was engrossed in the movie.

Even though the movie, Pretty Woman, was really old and she'd seen it at least a dozen times before, she didn't notice when it became night outside and was surprised by the sound of her family coming home. Her mother looked in to the living room and turned on the light. "Hey, how was the movie?"

"Oh, good. You timed that well – it just ended as you got home."

"Great. You can help us unload then. We'll bring the stuff from the car and you can pack it away. How's that sound?"

"Sure, no problems." Larissa took the bags from her mother and made her way into the kitchen. Putting them on the counter she began unpacking and putting things away.

Her mother made them their first home-cooked dinner in their new home and then Larissa returned to painting her room. When she was about halfway through, her parents came in to say goodnight. Larissa kept painting. After completing the second coat on the walls, she got started on the trims. She'd chosen a glossy ebony colour and once it was completed she stepped back to take a look.

The room looked better than she'd hoped and much different from yesterday when she first saw it. Now it was starting to feel like it was really hers.

She couldn't sleep in there with the paint smell so she changed into her pyjamas, grabbed her sleeping bag and pillow and headed for the living room. The home theatre chairs were a perfect substitute for bed with their ability to recline, and she could watch the movie again and pretend it was Brandon coming to claim her.

27

SEVEN

The next morning Larissa woke early. Her parents were already up and in the kitchen. She joined them for breakfast. Today was her Dad's first day at work in the Adelaide office. He was just finishing his coffee as she sat down.

"Hey Lari. Did you get your room all done?"

"Yeah Dad. It smelled too much of paint so I slept in the living room. Should be okay now, but."

"That's good. Got any plans?"

"Not yet. Thought I might go check out the beach and see what the surf's like. Are you going to work today?"

"Yeah, honey. First day in the office." He smiled and looked at her still in her pyjamas. "You don't look dressed for surfing."

"I didn't say I was going to go surfing right now, Dad." Larissa smiled back at him. "I just thought I'd go have a look at the beach and see if anyone was surfing there. Besides, it won't take me long to have breakfast and get changed, y'know."

Her dad laughed, "I know, sweetie, I'm just teasing. Have a good day." He got up and stepped into the kitchen to give Deb a quick hug and kiss goodbye. "I'm off to work, love. See you tonight."

"Have a good day, Steve," Deb replied, turning to give him a quick kiss in return.

Larissa finished her cereal and juice and got up from the table. Entering her room she was hit by the smell of paint so she opened the window to let the room air. She grabbed her toiletries bag and then selected a bath sheet from the linen press. As her father's car pulled out of the drive, she slipped into the bathroom and showered.

Finished with her shower a short while later she dressed in her favourite black one-piece swimsuit with the gold links, covering it with a sheer black kaftan mini dress. Quickly she put on some waterproof foundation, rimming her eyes with thick black kohl and black mascara, and coating her lips in cherry gloss. She quickly braided her damp hair into a loose plait and pulled a black cotton baseball cap onto her head, her braid spilling out the back of the hat. Next she fastened a pair of flat-heeled black suede gladiator sandals to her feet. She grabbed her black messenger bag and tossed her wallet and phone into it, slinging it over her shoulder. Lastly, she found her favourite black sunglasses and rested them on top of the cap's brim. Larissa surveyed herself in one of the mirrored doors on her robe and satisfied with the result, headed out the front door, calling to her mother as she left, "I'm off to the beach, Mum! Got my phone and I'll be back soon."

She strolled down the aptly named Beach Road to the beach, pleased and surprised to discover their home was only two streets from the sand and surf. The sea was a beautiful dark blue-green and there were at least half a dozen surfers out in the waves. The waves weren't that big, but after watching the surfers for about ten minutes, Larissa was itching to be in the water with them so she got up from her spot on the sand and headed back home.

She went inside, calling to her mother, "Mum! I'm back to get my surfboard."

"Okay, honey. Come home before it gets dark, please."

Before she could answer, her brother, Brad, called out, "Hey, I wanna come too!"

Larissa was about to tell him no, but then she realized he could keep an eye on her wallet and clothes. "Okay," she told him, "but you have to keep an eye on my stuff."

"Yeah, I will. Thanks, Lari," he answered her, grabbing a towel for himself and running out the door ahead of her.

Larissa grabbed her surfboard in its silver bag from the back deck and followed Brad back to the beach. Quickly she pulled off her kaftan and sandals and hat and threw them down on the sand on top of her bag and the towel she'd also grabbed while she was at home. "Don't run off anywhere, okay?" she told him.

"I won't, sis," Brad answered. "But I can go in the water, can't I?"

"Sure, just don't go in too deep and make sure you keep an eye on our stuff, okay?"

"Yup," he told her. Taking her board out of its bag, she started for the water, joining the other surfers riding the small sets of waves. Brad followed her into the water, staying close to the shore and looking up to check on their belongings every few minutes.

A couple of hours after they got to the beach, Larissa got out of the water and joined Brad on the sand. "So, kiddo, wanna go home yet?"

"Nah, I'm okay," he told her. "But do ya reckon we could get some fish and chips from the shop? I'm kinda hungry."

"Yeah, that's not a bad idea," she told him. "Okay. You stay here and I'll go get us some fish and chips. Want vinegar or lemon?"

"Vinegar. Can we get some drinks, too?"

"Yeah. What do ya want?"

"Lemonade. Ta, Lari. You're a cool sister sometimes."

"Yeah. Don't suck up." Lari laughed and pulled her kaftan on over her swimsuit. "Wait here. I'll be back soon."

"Yup." Brad went back to working on the fortress-like sandcastle he was building. "I'll be right here."

EIGHT

Larissa walked up to the local takeaway and ordered two pieces of fish, a serve of chips, and two cans of drink. Returning from the shop where she'd bought the food, she noticed the same guy she'd bumped into at the library standing on the foreshore by the boat ramp near the Surf Lifesavers. He was too far away for her to see where he was looking but heart did the funny flip-flop thing again and once more she found herself wondering who he was.

She raced back to the beach with the food and drinks and sitting next to Brad, looked up towards the ramp, hoping to see the mysterious guy still standing there. To her disappointment, he'd left.

"Damn," she whispered.

"What, Lari?" asked her brother with a mouthful of food.

"Nothing. Eat."

The two siblings ate their lunch and then goofed off on the beach for a while. Larissa forgot about the dark-haired guy until a shadow appeared over them.

"Excuse me," she heard spoken with the English accent she recognised from the day before. Looking up, she saw the mysterious guy.

"Hey," she said in a nervous voice. "What's up?"

"You're the girl from the library, aren't you?"

"Yeah, that's me. You're the guy from the library."

"Yes."

"So..." Larissa didn't know what to say next. Brad was looking at each of them in turn, not saying anything yet.

"I saw you, when I was walking along the foreshore. That was you surfing?" He waved in the general direction of the water where she'd been riding the waves.

"Yeah, I guess so. I was surfing before," she pointed at her board, standing in the sand. "That's my board."

"I thought it was. Nice board. What is it? A Glen Winton quad?"

"Yeah. Do you know much about surfing?" Larissa was impressed that he knew what her board was.

"Some. I could be better. You looked good out there."

Larissa decided that she really liked his accent. She was trying to get a really good look at him without appearing to stare. She realized he was very pale, much paler than she'd thought when she bumped into him at the library. Clearly he didn't do that much surfing or he'd have at least some kind of light tan unless he did all his surfing in a steamer or at night. "Oh, thanks." She

31

didn't know what to say next. "Ummmnn... I'm Lari and this is my brother, Brad." She pointed at Brad as she introduced them.

"Larry?" he asked, looking confused.

"L-A-R-I," she spelled it for him. "It's short for Larissa, but I hate that."

"Oh," he smiled at them. "Hi Lari. Hi Brad. I'm Dante."

"Hiya," said Brad. He looked at Larissa, "I'm bored now so I'm gonna go home, Lari. Is that okay?"

"Sure, Brad, but straight home, okay? Do you know the way?" Brad nodded and left and Larissa continued, looking at Dante, "Dante? Wow, I've never met anyone called Dante before."

He shrugged, "It's an old family name." Still smiling, he continued, "I've never met a girl called Lari before, either."

"Ha. You got me," she answered, laughing. "So, you're not in school then, Dante?"

"Sort of. I'm at uni. Classes are finished for today."

"Oh, cool. Your accent's English, isn't it?"

"Yes. My family's from England."

"Are they here too?"

"No. I share a house with some friends."

He seemed uncomfortable with the questions, so Larissa continued, "Oh. I'm being nosy. You can tell me to piss off, if you want."

He laughed. "No, you don't have to piss off." He paused, "So, I came over because I wanted to say sorry for bumping into you at the library and ask if you were new here. I haven't seen you around before."

"You don't have to say sorry. You didn't bump into me. I wasn't looking and I bumped into you. And yeah, we just moved here. I start school next week."

"School?" He seemed surprised to hear she was in school. "What year are you in?"

"Year 10." Larissa wrinkled her nose. "I don't know if I'm gonna like school here much. It looks heaps different to what I'm used to."

"Oh, really?" Dante sat down on the sand beside her. "Where are you from then?"

"Sydney. I went to a girls' school. Now I'm gonna be going to Christies Beach High. It's co-ed."

"So schools are different in Sydney?"

"Yeah. Heaps. They seem to be, anyway." Larissa tried to look at him some more without being noticed. His eyes were rimmed with silky black lashes; the whites looked sparkling bright, making his pale blue-green irises stand out. She realized again that his skin was incredibly pale. Except that his hair

32

and eyelashes were so dark she would've assumed he was albino. Again her heart did a strange flip-flop. "What are you studying at uni?"

"Philosophy."

"Philosophy?"

"Yes. It's something that interests me."

"Really?" Larissa was stumped. She wanted to keep him talking but she didn't know how to continue the conversation.

"Yes. Do you know what you plan to do when you're finished with school?"

"Nah..." Larissa smiled at him. "I haven't given it a lot of thought, really. My 'rents give me grief over it but I just don't know what I wanna do."

"Well, you have time to figure out what you like." He stared out over the sea.

"Yeah, I guess." Larissa decided that his smile was one of the things making her heart flip-flop and wished he'd smile at her again. "How'd you know you wanted to do philosophy?"

"Oh, it was just something I found interesting." Abruptly, he stood. "Well, Lari. I have to get moving. Things I have to do."

"Oh, okay," Larissa realized she sounded disappointed.

He looked at her and she couldn't read his expression. "Maybe we'll see each other again soon."

"Yeah. That'd be cool." Larissa thought quickly. "I'll probably be here again tomorrow if the surf's okay. I only live just up the road." She waved her hand in the direction of her new home.

"Really?" He looked in the direction she'd pointed, and then back to her face. "I'm here at the beach a lot too. We live just over there." He pointed at a double storey house to the south on the cliffs overlooking the beach, surrounded by a wall-like fence.

"Wow. Nice house."

"Yes. It's okay." He paused, looking in the direction of his own house, and then turned to face Larissa. "Well, I might see you here again then, Lari."

"Yup, maybe," she winked at him.

Dante grinned at her, "I'll see you soon, then," he told her. "Bye, Lari."

"Yeah, see you soon, Dante." Larissa watched him walk along the beach towards the house on the cliffs and when he'd gone halfway to the house, she pulled her board out of the sand, tossed it into its bag and headed back home. She didn't look back or she would've seen him stop and turn to watch her leave.

NINE

Lari arrived home to discover Brad had already told her mother about meeting Dante at the beach.

"Who's this boy Brad told me about, Lari?" She didn't wait for an answer before continuing, "He says he wasn't in school. How old is he? He's not too old for you to be hanging around with, is he?"

"Oh, Mum, please!" Lari groaned. "We met at the library yesterday when I bumped into him and then he saw me at the beach and said hi. It's no big deal." She rolled her eyes and got a drink out of the fridge. "And I don't know how old he is coz I never asked. He looks about seventeen or eighteen, I guess. He's from England and he's at uni... doing philosophy, he said."

"Oh." Her mother didn't seem to know what else to say. She looked at Brad who was looking interested in the exchange. "Brad described you as 'making goo-goo eyes' at him and I guess I might've jumped the gun a bit."

"Mum! Goo-goo eyes? That sounds disgusting." Larissa rolled her eyes again and turned on Brad, "And don't bother asking to come to the beach with me again if you're gonna make up shit like that, idiot brother! Is that why you said you wanted to go home? So you could tell stupid bullshit lies?"

"Larissa! Language! And don't talk to your brother like that. Apologise please," her mother reprimanded.

"No," Larissa felt rebellious. "I won't. He should apologise for making stuff up. Dante and I were just talking and that's all. He was talking to Brad, too, till Brad said he wanted to go home and left."

"Dante?" Her mother was distracted by the name. "What an unusual name. Is that this boy's name then?"

"Yes. And he lives in that really cool house on the top of the cliffs." Larissa decided she'd had enough of this conversation. "I'm going to read now," she told her mother and departed for her room.

Alone in her room, Larissa sprawled on her bed with the book she'd borrowed from the library open in front of her. She stared at the page but she wasn't reading, she was remembering her conversation with Dante and trying to remember every little detail about him.

"Goo-goo eyes," she muttered to herself. "I wasn't making goo-goo eyes at him." But even while she was denying it, she knew that she thought he was incredibly attractive. There was something almost hypnotic about him.

She got up and slipped her iPod into the speaker dock, turning it on. You Took, her favourite song by The Church, started playing. The lyrics, "You took a piece of my heart..." seemed kind of prophetic. For the second time since she moved to Adelaide she'd forgotten about Brandon and the only face she was imagining was Dante's.

Larissa sprawled on her bed again; book in front of her in case her mother decided to check on her but her mind was miles away. She stared at her reflection in the mirror and wondered if Dante was interested in her or if he just saw a schoolgirl and thought she was too young for him.

The song ended and Larissa jumped off the bed and wandered into the kitchen to grab the cordless phone. "Hey, I'm gonna ring Ebony if that's okay? I haven't talked to her since we got here."

"All right, but no more than an hour, okay?" her mother answered.

"Yup. I'm taking the phone into my room so just knock on the door when my hour's up, okay?"

"Will do." Her mother was prepping dinner and Brad had vanished. Larissa could hear the muffled sound of the TV and figured that Brad was in the living room watching something.

When she returned to her room, Low Happening by The Howling Bells was halfway through. She turned the volume down a little and dialled Ebony. The phone rang a few times and then her friend answered.

"Hey, Ebony! It's Lari."

"Lari!" Ebony sounded excited. "How's Adelaide? What's your house like? Do you have a cool room? Have you made any new friends yet?"

"Whoa! One question at a time!" Larissa laughed. "Okay, house is all right... a bit bigger than our old place, I guess. Dad's turned one of the living rooms into a kind of home theatre. My room's bigger than my old one and I painted it blue coz it was all white and it's got this huge built-in robe that goes the length of one wall and half the doors are like mirrors..."

"Awesome! What about friends? Have you been to your new school yet?"

"Kind of. Mum and I drove past it the second day we were here. The school's huge. It's like two campuses."

"Serious? Two? Wow."

"Yeah, but I don't start there till Monday so I haven't actually been there yet." Larissa paused. "But I kinda met this guy..."

"A guy?" Ebony gushed, "Tell me more... Is he cute? Does he go to your new school? Your new school is co-ed, right? You said it was gonna be..."

"Hang on!" Larissa laughed. "Yeah, the school's co-ed but he doesn't go there. He's at uni."

"Uni? How'd you meet a uni guy?"

"I bumped into him at the library and then today when I was surfing down the beach he was there." Larissa remembered how close the beach was.

35

"Hey, you wouldn't believe how close the beach is to our house. It's awesome! I can just walk down the road to go for a surf."

"Yeah, that's great about the beach. Now tell me more about this guy. C'mon, is he cute? And what's his name? How old is he? You haven't told me anything!" she wailed with a giggle in her voice. "And did you really meet him at the library?"

'Arrghh... His name's Dante and he's really, really cute. He's like, I dunno, about six feet tall or a bit more I guess... he's heaps taller than me, anyway... and he's kinda skinny but not scrawny... muscular like a runner, maybe... and he has really pale skin and dark hair and the most startling eyes. And yeah, I walked straight into him at the library. I felt like an idiot when I did it."

"Oh, he sounds gorgeous... What a weird name, but... Is that really his name?" Like an afterthought, she added, "Why did you feel like an idiot?"

"Coz I didn't see him and I just slammed straight into him. And yeah, that is his name. I like it. Oh, and I nearly forgot! He's from England and he has the most fantastic accent!"

"Serious? Oh, awesome! So, has he asked you out or anything?"

"No! But I think I'm gonna see him again. I told him I was gonna be surfing again tomorrow so I think he's gonna show up. He lives in this totally awesome looking house on the top of the cliffs by the beach. It's got all these windows and decks and it looks kinda like it belongs in Hollywood."

"Oooh, really? Oh, you have to call me again tomorrow night to tell me what happens or I'll die!"

Larissa laughed, "You will not! But I'll call ya anyway." The conversation switched to all the stuff that had happened to Ebony and Sera since Larissa left and before she knew it, her mother was knocking on the door.

"Lari, your hour's up and dinner's about five minutes away."

"Okay, Mum, I'm hanging up now," she told her mother before saying goodbye to Ebony. "I'll ring you again tomorrow, okay? Bye," she told her friend before hanging up and joining her family for dinner.

TEN

Early the next morning Larissa got up and dressed in her white printed one-piece, pulling on a pair of denim cut-off shorts and a white mesh tank top over the swimsuit. She dug out her white patent flat gladiator sandals, found a soft white cotton cap and did her make-up carefully, hooking her sunglasses into the neck of her tank.

Finally, she splashed some vanilla oil on her wrists and neck. Satisfied with the result, she grabbed her surfboard and told her mother she was spending the day at the beach.

Brad was still in his room when she left so she was saved from having to take him with her. Larissa was still mad at him for telling her mother about Dante yesterday and didn't want him hanging around, especially as she was hoping to see Dante again.

"Who's going to the beach with you, Lari?" her mother asked as she was collecting her board.

"No-one, Mum. I wanna spend the day surfing. I'll be back at school next week and I won't be able to spend the whole day surfing except for weekends."

"Okay. Home before dark, please."

"No worries. See ya," she called as she bailed out the door, surfboard in its bag and slung over her right shoulder, messenger tote and towel over her left. The sun was dazzling and she slipped her sunglasses on as she walked out the front gate.

Her heart was thumping and she realized she was feeling kind of nervous but when she got to the beach and scanned it for any sign of Dante, she was disappointed to discover that he wasn't there.

The waves were better today though, so she stripped down to her swimsuit and piled her things in a heap on the sand and dived into the waves. Today she'd brought her waterproof phone holder that also carried her money so she wouldn't have to risk leaving any valuables alone on the beach. With her money and phone safely clipped to her hip she could relax and enjoy the waves.

Time passed quickly and after a while she realized she was getting hungry. Lari stuck her board in the sand and pulling her tank and shorts back on over her wet swimsuit, slipped her hat on over her wet hair, and shielded her eyes with her sunglasses. Slinging her board into its bag, she headed up to the takeaway to buy some lunch. Today she bought a serve of salt & pepper squid and some chips and a milkshake and took it back to her spot on the sand.

37

She didn't mean to stare at the house he'd pointed out as his, but since there wasn't much else to draw her attention and Dante was on her mind, she found her eyes wandering in that direction.

From the beach the house looked like something out of a magazine that some celebrity would live in. The fence was a solid wall and really high and seemed to go all the way round. Behind the wall, all she could see of the house was the upper level and it had lots of glass and decks. She couldn't see in, but she could see the sun reflecting off the windows.

She checked the time on her phone and was surprised to discover it was nearly three o'clock. Since her mother's idea of getting home before dark actually meant getting home before her father got home from work, Lari knew she only had another two or three hours of surfing time left and quickly stripped back down to her swimsuit for another turn in the water.

Clipping her phone and cash back onto her hip, she grabbed her board and walked back into the sea, paddling out into the waves and surfing for another couple of hours. The sun was well on its way down when she finally got out of the water. She stopped at the water's edge, forgetting to breathe for a few seconds when she realized Dante was sitting on the sand beside her pile of clothes. Then she took a deep breath and smiled at him, walking faster to join him.

"Hey," she greeted him.

"Hey," he answered, smiling back at her.

"I thought you weren't gonna be here today..." her voice faded as she decided not to say anymore along that line of thought.

"Uni. I'm done for the day now."

"Oh, cool." She wedged her board in the sand and sat on her towel beside him. "Yeah, I've been surfing most of the day. Waves have been good. Better than yesterday."

"I saw you... for the last five or ten minutes. You really look great out there."

Larissa felt herself blushing. "Aww, thanks. You said that yesterday. I'll get embarrassed if ya keep saying stuff like that."

"Sorry," he grinned at her and she knew he wasn't really.

"So, now you get to the beach and I'm just about to go home..."

"Oh, really?" He looked at her like he was unsure.

"Yeah, my mum's got this thing about me having to get home before Dad gets home from work and he gets home about six or six-thirty and it's gotta be close to that now..."

"Oh." He looked out to sea. "I think it's nearly six now."

"Well, it only takes me about five minutes to walk up the street, so I've got another ten or fifteen to hang here."

He looked at her and smiled. Immediately she felt her heart do that crazy flip-flop and for a second she forgot how to breathe again. "Damn, you have a killer smile!" she told him, and then looked shocked. "Oh, I didn't mean to say that out loud!" Now she was blushing furiously and staring at the sand.

"Hey, thanks... You're cute when you blush like that y'know."

"Oh, shut up!" she told him, but not really meaning it. Lari looked up at him again and smiled. "I've probably gotta get going..."

"Yeah. Are you going to be here again tomorrow?"

"Probably. I don't have anything else planned."

"I have morning classes, but I'll probably get here about four or four-thirty. I'll see you then... If you're here."

"Okay. See you then."

"Okay." They both stood up and Lari started dressing to leave. He watched and waited till she was nearly done. She wasn't watching him so she didn't see him put her board in its bag but by the time she was dressed, her board was packed away and he was holding it. He walked her up to the roadside and then handed her board over. "See you tomorrow, Lari."

"See ya, Dante." They both stood and smiled at each other. "If I don't go, I'll be late..."

"Go!" He laughed. "I'll see you tomorrow afternoon."

"Okay, bye!"

"Bye."

Lari started walking up the street, looking behind once to see him still standing there smiling at her. He really made her heart go crazy, pounding like mad but in a good way. She smiled all the way home.

"You look happy," her mother greeted her as she walked inside.

"Yeah, great day surfing. Think I'll go again tomorrow, if that's okay."

"Sure. Go put your stuff away and wash up for dinner. Your Dad's pulling in the drive now."

Lari did as she was told, unable to stop smiling.

ELEVEN

The next morning Larissa was up early and ready for her day at the beach. Even though she knew Dante wouldn't arrive until late in the afternoon, it didn't stop her wanting to enjoy the day surfing.

It wasn't quite as bright and sunny as the day before and the forecasters were predicting cloudy skies and rain for the rest of the week so Lari figured she should get out and enjoy the water today in case it got squally and no good for surfing when the weather changed.

She didn't mind hitting the water in the rain but her mother could be funny about it. And if the sea was choppy and didn't have decent waves, it wouldn't be any good for surfing anyway.

Today she packed her digital camera in her messenger bag since she'd promised Ebony on the phone last night that she'd try to get a photo of Dante to send to her. The internet still wasn't connected to their new house yet but it was supposed to be happening before the end of the week so she'd agreed to send the photo to Ebony once she was online again.

She wore her black swimsuit again today, with her favourite denim cut-off shorts and a black lace tank over it. Her black baseball cap was parked on her head and today she'd braided her long blonde curls into a loose plait. Although she'd let her hair hang loose yesterday, the simple braid was her preferred hairstyle when she was intent on surfing. Her favourite black sunglasses were perched on her hat and her black gladiators were on her feet.

Larissa had stuck to her usual simple look of waterproof foundation, black kohl and mascara and cherry lip-gloss, dabbing vanilla oil on her wrists and behind her ears.

She hadn't forgotten that Dante had called her cute yesterday, even if he'd been referring to her blushing. Tomorrow was Friday and she was hoping he'd ask her to go out somewhere with him on the weekend.

Her mother seemed to have forgotten about Dante since she hadn't asked about him again and Larissa figured she'd say nothing about him either unless she had to. Brad was spending the day with her mother doing some shopping so Lari was off the hook on babysitting him. Everything seemed to be working out for her.

She was at the beach and in the water before lunchtime and spent the next few hours riding the waves. The waves weren't any better than the day before, but there were a few more surfers out there and she ended up meeting and hanging with a few of them for a while.

Thommo and Zac were two seventeen year old surfers who told her they'd quit high school and were supposed to be at TAFE doing their mechanic apprenticeship training but they'd decided to skip for the day and catch some waves. Their girlfriends, Lisa and Melanie were with them. The girls were just turned sixteen and in the same year as Lari. Both girls were supposed to be at Christies Beach High but they were skipping off school to hang with their boyfriends for the day.

"I'm starting at Christies Beach High on Monday," Lari informed them.

"Really? Oh so cool! I'll show you around. Maybe we'll even be in some of the same classes!" Melanie exclaimed. "Lisa and I don't bail off all that often. Just sometimes when the boys take the day off and we all go surfing."

"Aren't you afraid of getting busted?" Lari asked.

"Nah, not really. Lisa's 'rents both work and they're gone before she needs to leave for school and they don't come home till way after school ends so I go to her place and get changed there."

Around three o'clock the foursome had to leave so they could keep up the illusion of having been to school so Lari swapped addresses and phone numbers with the girls and they all said goodbye, promising to catch up on the weekend before school started on Monday.

Larissa went back into the water after they'd left and caught a few more waves, stepping out about four o'clock to discover Dante already on the beach, sitting beside her clothes, watching her surf.

The sight of him took her breath away again. "How do you do that?" she asked as she walked up to him.

"Do what?" he answered.

"Just appear there. I swear I looked up before and you weren't there and then you just were."

Dante laughed. "I don't know. Maybe you just don't notice me till I sit down next to your stuff."

"Hmmmnn... maybe." She sounded unconvinced. "I think I'd notice you anywhere, though."

He laughed again. "Thanks. I think. You did mean that in a good way?"

Lari laughed too, sitting down beside him, "Yeah, I meant it in a good way."

"Good day surfing?"

"Yeah, it was, actually. I met some girls from school."

"Really? Shouldn't they have been at school?"

Lari half-frowned as she looked at him, "You aren't going to turn into my mother now, are you?"

Dante laughed. "Not likely!"

41

Larissa continued, "Yeah, they were skipping for the day to catch some waves with their boyfriends. It's all good. How was your day?"

"Usual. Classes in the morning. Here now. Nothing really exciting to report."

"Oh," she sat and stared out over the sea, wondering how to get a photo of him and where to go with the conversation.

"I have the whole day off tomorrow. Are you going to be here again?"

"Oh, I dunno." Larissa immediately wanted desperately to spend the day on the beach tomorrow. "The weather report's cloud and rain and my mother can get funny about me heading to the beach when it's like that."

"Oh, okay."

They both sat silent for a few minutes. Larissa was twitching, her mind frantically trying to work out how she could promise to be at the beach, even if the weather was crap and her mother forbade it.

"I like the beach when it's rainy," Dante continued into the silence. "It's different."

"Yeah, I kind of like the sea then, too," Larissa added. "Oh, y'know what? I'm gonna be here, even if the weather's crap, okay?"

"Are you sure? I mean, I don't want you to think I'm trying to make you, or anything."

"Yeah, right. I'm kind of wilful. People aren't usually very successful at making me do anything." Larissa laughed as she spoke and Dante grinned back at her. "Oh, I love your smile!" Straight away she blushed. "Oh, crap! I didn't mean to say that!"

"I love it when you blush," Dante replied.

"Shut up!" she laughingly told him. "Hey, I'm curious. How old are you?"

"Me?" he paused. "Nineteen. How old are you?"

"Fifteen," she paused, "Sixteen in a couple of months."

"Fifteen?" He blinked and looked out over the sea.

"Nearly sixteen."

"Nearly sixteen, hey?" He grinned at her. "You seem older somehow."

"Older? How much older?"

"Oh, first time I saw you I thought you were at least sixteen, I guess," he laughed.

"Well, I'm only a couple of months younger than you thought I was and don't make fun of me." Larissa pouted, frowning at Dante.

He raised an eyebrow as he looked at her, "There is that way of looking at it and I wasn't making fun of you. Really." He tried to look contrite but failed and just managed to look mischievous instead.

"Yeah, just look at it that way," she smiled at him. She decided it was too hard to sneak a photo of him and she wasn't going to ask either so Ebony could wait for her picture of Dante. "So, you're gonna meet me here at the beach tomorrow then?"

"Yeah, I guess I am. Ten o'clock too early?"

"Nah, sounds good. Want me to bring my board or not?"

"If you want. I like watching you surf and I might bring my board and do some surfing, too. If the waves are any good."

"Hey, that'd be cool. So you do surf then?"

"Yeah. Not much, though. I like night surfing."

"Figures." He raised his eyebrows as he looked at her and Larissa continued, "Well you are kind of pale-skinned. Doesn't really scream at me that you spend much time in the sun."

"I'm English."

"Yeah, but you are really pale." She smiled because he looked uncomfortable. "Anyway, I think you look pretty hot. That pale skin and those eyes are just awesome." She looked shocked as he smiled. "Oh hell, why did I tell you that?"

He shrugged and smiled at her. "It's cool. You're pretty awesome yourself. So, tomorrow at ten o'clock here on the beach."

"Yup, that's the plan." Larissa wanted to leap about with excitement and pleasure but restrained herself to a blushing smile.

"Okay," he stood up. "Well, I better get going now. I've got a bit of stuff to do if I'm gonna spend tomorrow hanging out with you."

"Yeah, I should head home too," Larissa agreed as she stood and started packing up her things. He walked her up to the roadside again, handing her the board as she said goodbye, "See you tomorrow, Dante."

"Yeah, see you tomorrow, Lari."

She smiled and walked up the road towards home, looking back once to see him staring after her, just like yesterday. Her heart did the crazy flip-flop thing again and she grinned even more. Tomorrow she was spending the day with him. Life was looking good and maybe Adelaide wasn't so bad, after all.

TWELVE

Larissa could hardly contain herself when she woke up. It was only eight o'clock, so she had two hours to fill before she met Dante at the beach. If she'd thought she could do it without being noticed, she would've skipped breakfast since there seemed to be a flock of butterflies rampaging in her stomach, but her mother wasn't unobservant enough to let that slip by her.

So Larissa ate a piece of toast and an apple, washing them down with a mug of coffee. It was cloudy outside but not windy and not yet raining so she was hopeful that the waves would be okay.

"Hey Mum, since today is the last school day I can spend at the beach, I wanna surf. Is that cool?" She wanted to just tell her mother that she was going to the beach but she felt nervous that her mother would somehow be able to tell that she was meeting Dante.

"Really? You want to surf in this weather? It looks like it's going to rain, Lari," her mother answered, sounding doubtful.

"Mum, you know I like surfing in the rain too."

"I really don't understand that, Lari, but I understand your desire to spend your last free school day surfing, so okay. If a storm develops though, I want you to come straight home, understood?"

"Sure. I can do that. Thanks, Mum. I'm gonna have a shower and get dressed and then I'm off," Lari bolted from the room, anxious to get to the beach before her mother changed her mind.

Today she dressed in her white one-piece swimsuit and threw a white fringed long t-shirt style mini-dress over it, pulling her white gladiator sandals on her feet. Since it was so grey and cloudy outside, she didn't bother with a hat and she left her hair loose, but she did add sunglasses, just to complete the look she was after.

Larissa had about an hour to spare once she was done getting ready. She was so nervous that her mother would somehow figure out that she was meeting Dante and forbid her to go that she grabbed her board and left early.

"Going now, Mum. Got my phone if you need me."

"Okay, Lari. Remember, come home straight away if a storm blows up," her mother paused before adding, "Be careful."

"Yeah, I will. See ya later." Larissa was already out the door as she called her farewell. She could feel the relief as she walked out the gate and headed to the beach.

Brad hated rainy days at the beach so at least she was spared trying to avoid taking him. He probably wouldn't even get out of bed till she was already

44

with Dante. The more she thought of Dante's name, the more she liked it and him.

The waves weren't the greatest, but at least the sea wasn't choppy so Lari stripped down to her swimsuit and surfed, trying to keep an eye on the beach. She didn't notice him until he was standing beside her gear with a board next to him. Quickly she got out of the water to join him.

"Really, it's amazing how you do that. I was watching for you and yet I never saw you till you were standing there."

He shrugged. "You weren't watching all the time. You were surfing too. Pretty good surfing, actually."

She grinned. "Don't change the subject." Then she noticed his board. "Hey, that's a cool board."

"You think so?" He looked at his board as if he was just seeing it for the first time. "I've had it ages, although I don't really use it much."

"Yeah? That's a Dick Brewer swallowtail from the seventies, isn't it? I'd kill for one of those."

"You know your boards," he told her. Then he smiled. "You'd kill for my board? Really? Am I safe here now?" he laughed.

"Yeah, today you are," she laughed in reply. "I wanna do some surfing with you, so I better let you keep that board. And your life."

"Thanks! So, shall we surf?"

"Yup. Race ya in," she picked up her board and started running for the water. Just as she started wading, he strode past her, grinning wildly.

They surfed for the next hour or so, finally making their way back onto the sand, just as the rain started to drizzle down.

"My mum says I have to go straight home if a storm blows up, so cross your fingers that doesn't happen, okay?" she told him as they sat on the beach.

"Fingers crossed." He looked at the sky. "I think we're safe from storms. Rain's another story. I think that might be here to stay."

"Yeah. Rain's okay. Mum only mentioned storms."

"Very specific."

"She can be." Larissa decided to change the subject. "So, how long have you been in Oz?"

"Oh, a couple of years. I've got one more year left on my degree."

"One more year?"

"Yeah. Not sure where I'm headed after that. Might stick around and do some post-grad study."

"Cool. What's uni like?"

"Pretty good. Lots of study. Interesting. What's high school like?"

"Ha! Good question. Back home in Sydney, it was pretty good. I had mates I grew up with since we were little kids and I knew how it all worked. I feel out of place here. Don't know how it works or anything or anybody so I'm kinda scared, I guess." She paused and remembered the girls she'd met the day before. "Well, I suppose I've met some of the girls who go there... but we've only met once so it's not really the same as having friends."

"I'm sure you'll be fine." He looked into her eyes and her heart went crazy again. "You are very likable, y'know."

"Oh gee, thanks." Larissa was blushing. "Why do you always make me blush?"

"Hmmnn... Don't know, but I like it when you do." He smiled at her. "More surfing?"

"Sure." She jumped up and grabbed her board, racing for the water. Even with her head start he overtook her just as she started wading in, grinning at her again. "Grrrr!" she growled at him as he beat her.

"Now, now!" he remonstrated, not pausing to stop, his killer smile taking her breath away again.

She jumped on her board and started paddling to join him and they surfed for the next hour or so. Even though he'd told her he hardly surfed, she could see he was really good and wished she could be sitting on the beach watching him, the way he'd watched her. But she liked surfing with him too and she couldn't have it both ways.

THIRTEEN

They sat on the beach again in the rain for another half hour or so until Larissa's stomach started to voice its hunger loudly.

"Is that you?" Dante asked her with a mischievous look on his face.

"Yes." Lari was mortified. She was trying to be cool around him and a growling stomach didn't seem very cool. "I think I need feeding." The only response she could think of was humour. Right now she was wishing she'd eaten a hearty breakfast.

"Wait here and I'll be right back."

"Okay…" Lari wasn't sure what he was up to but she figured she'd do what he asked. A short while later he was back with some hot chips and a can of drink.

"Food for the hungry girl," he told her, handing her the cup of chips and can.

"Thanks," she took them from him and started eating. "What about you?"

"Oh, I have this weird thing about not eating junk food."

"But you'll feed it to me," she laughed. "Gee, thanks, I think."

He laughed with her. "I've seen you eating plenty of it down here."

"Ha! How do you know that? Have you been spying on me?"

He looked startled. "No! I mean, I've just seen you eating takeaway and drinking cans of soft drink down here a few times."

"Yeah, right… I'll let you off this time…" she smiled to let him know she was still joking around. "So, are we spending the rest of the afternoon surfing or do ya wanna do something else?"

"What would be the something else? Do you have something in mind?" He looked relieved at the change of subject.

"Well, no, actually. I was kind of hoping you might."

"I suppose I could show you around since the only place I think you've been is the beach."

"And Colonnades. And the library," she added with a grin.

"Oh, well travelled!" he laughed. "Okay. Do you want to leave your board at my place and then we can take a walk along the cliffs?"

"Sure, sounds great."

She finished eating and then they packed up their boards and walked along the beach to his house on the cliffs. They entered through a big wooden gate and Lari was impressed by the beautiful garden and lawn between the fence and the house.

"Wow. This is a very cool place."

"Yeah, it's not bad." He pointed to a small storage alcove adjacent the wall-like fence. "Put your board here." He parked his board in the alcove and she did the same. "So, ready to explore?" he asked.

"Yup. Lead the way." Lari smiled.

He opened the gate and waved her through, following immediately. "This way." He pointed along the cliffs. "There's a great view from over here."

"Awesome." She walked alongside him as he led the way along the cliffs. The rain was light and misty but constant and after they'd walked in it for about five minutes, she started to feel soaked through and slightly cold.

Dante glanced at her. "You're shivering. Are you cold?" he asked.

"Oh, a little bit. I'm okay, but."

"Here, take my jacket." He removed his light waterproof jacket and draped it over her.

"Now you'll be cold," she told him. He was wearing only a grey t-shirt and his board shorts.

"Nah, I'm okay. I don't really feel the cold much." He paused. "English, remember? It's colder there."

"Yeah, right," she told him disbelievingly, but she didn't hand back the jacket. Already she felt warmer with it draped around her. She slipped her arms into the sleeves and zipped it up. A few minutes later they were at the top of the cliffs and she turned to look back towards town. The view took her breath away. "Oh, that's just awesome. Wow."

"Yeah, I thought you'd like it." He pointed towards the town. "You can pretty much see most of Christies Beach from here. Kind of an overview." She looked where he was pointing.

She glanced back at his home. "You'd have pretty similar views from your house."

"Yeah. Pretty much." He paused. "Did you know where we're standing now is called Witton Bluff? It used to be called Pointe Picturesque and then in the 1800s a ship owned by a guy called Witton crashed into the cliffs and its name changed to Witton Bluff."

"Really? How do you know this stuff?"

"I like history."

"That's pretty cool. Know any other history stories you wanna share?"

"Yeah, I could take you sightseeing some day, maybe. There's lots of places here on the Fleurieu Peninsula that have great stories to them. And then there's the Barossa Valley in the north."

"That would be awesome." He was standing close behind her so she decided to take the opportunity to step back slightly and lean against him. She decided he was more muscular than he looked because he felt like a rock and he must've been lying about feeling the cold since she could feel a chill emanating from him.

He was really still for a moment and then slowly slipped his arms around her. Lari closed her eyes and sighed with pleasure. "Sure you don't want your jacket back? I can tell you're cold."

"Nah. Told you, I'm tough. I can handle it." His voice sounded a little rougher than usual. He removed his arms and propelled her away from him, pointing her back the way they'd come. "C'mon, time to walk back."

"Hey, I don't have to be home till dark, y'know. It's not curfew time yet!"

"Yeah, but a storm's coming in and didn't you say you had to go home if a storm blew up?"

"Oh really?" she turned to look out over the water. A line of dark thundery clouds was heading their way. "Oh, bugger. Yeah, I better go home before that hits."

She started walking back. Without warning, she slipped on a wet patch of grass. "Shit!" she cried out as she felt herself falling. Before she could land on the hard ground, he'd caught her and pulled her to her feet. "Oh, thanks!" she told him. "Thought I was gonna land on my arse then or slide down the cliff."

"Not this time," he smiled at her. Her face was inches from his and as she stared into his pale eyes, her heart skipped. Seconds later, she felt his chilled lips against hers. Her heart went crazy as he took her breath away.

The kiss was brief but intense and she gasped, "Oh, do that again!" as he pulled away.

He laughed and his voice was throaty as he answered her, "Not today. It's wet and that storm's on its way in and you need to get home before you get into trouble."

She pouted, "Okay, but you're gonna do that again another time."

He laughed again and taking her hand, started leading her back to his house. "Yes, but not today. C'mon, you have to hurry," he insisted.

She could hear the rumble of thunder and realized that the storm was moving in fast. "Oh, so not fair," she muttered to herself under her breath. "Okay, I'm moving," she told him more loudly as he tugged on her hand.

They arrived at his gate just as a bolt of lightning streaked across the sky. "Oh, that's beautiful," she gushed, staring at the sky and forgetting to walk.

"Yeah, and if you ever wanna be let out to see me again, you'd better get home now and watch it from there."

"Spoilsport," she told him, pouting. "One more kiss before I go?" she asked, trying to look flirty.

He laughed, and lightly kissed her. It wasn't as intense as their first kiss, but she felt her body tingle with pleasure. He released her and handed her board to her. "Home, beautiful witch," he told her.

"Okay. But I want to know when you're gonna take me sightseeing." Lari wasn't leaving until he made another date with her.

"Soon, but not if you don't get home now," he gently pushed her out the gate. "Be good. I promise we'll see each other again. You've bewitched me, you beautiful girl." Quickly he brushed his cold lips against hers one more time, before propelling her out the gate more firmly.

"Okay," she reluctantly started backing away from him. "Only coz you promise and coz my mother will kill me if I don't get home now."

"Bye, Lari." He stood in the gateway, smiling at her.

"Hey," she said. "I still have your jacket on!"

"Keep it and give it back to me next time," he told her.

She smiled, feeling like next time was guaranteed now that she was holding something of his. "Okay. Bye Dante."

"Bye."

She spun and started walking faster back to her place, realizing that the storm was moving in very quickly and the rain was getting heavier as they'd talked.

She made it in her front door just before the full fury of the storm crashed down, slipping into her room first to remove Dante's jacket before her mother spied her in it.

FOURTEEN

Larissa woke from a dream where Dante was kissing her with cold lips while rain fell on them. She sighed and kept her eyes closed, hoping to keep the dream alive a little longer. It didn't work.

Reluctantly, she opened her eyes and sat up, looking out the window to see that the rain was still pouring. "No, no, no. Not fair," she moaned softly. Thunder rumbled and she knew the storm was still about. "Go away, stupid storm," she muttered. "You're ruining my love life."

Lari got up and pulled her white towelling bathrobe on over the blue satin pyjamas she was wearing. There was even a bit of a chill still in the air, making it feel more like winter. Spring was still technically a few weeks away but she wanted its weather now. Just to finish her mood off, her head throbbed ominously, like there was the beginning of a headache waiting to happen.

She wandered out to the kitchen where her dad was eating breakfast while her mother made coffee.

"Hi sleepyhead. No surfing today in this weather," her dad greeted her. "Is that the reason for the sour face?"

"Hi Dad. Yup. I thought the storm would've blown over by now. And I've got a bit of a headache."

"Oh well. Take some Panadol for your head and remember, you can't control the weather, sweetie. The weather report says it should ease off today so you could probably surf again tomorrow."

"Yeah," Larissa sat at the table and leaned her head on her hands.

"Cereal? Toast? What would you like, Lari?"

"Cereal, thanks. And juice. And Panadol."

Her mother set about getting her breakfast ready and depositing it and a glass of water with two Panadol fizzing in it in front of her while her dad finished up. "Okay, I'm off to wake up Brad." He stood up and looked at Lari and then her mother. "Lari, maybe you'd like to go with your mother today. She's buying a second car since I need ours to drive to work each day. You could help her pick something."

Lari drank the Panadol and looked up, startled. "Yeah, that would be okay." She turned to her mother, "What are you getting?"

"Not sure yet, Lari. It's a terrible day for car shopping but I need something before Monday. Your father's taking us to some strip where there's miles of car yards. I'll call him if he needs to pick us up, but I'm sure we'll find something we like."

51

"Is Brad coming with us?"

"No, he's staying with your dad."

"Cool. Girls day out, hey Mum," Lari smiled.

Her mother returned the smile. "Yes, girls day out." She paused and then continued, "So, if you want to eat up, get showered and dressed, we can go. Your dad's waking Brad now."

"Okay," Lari shovelled the last of her breakfast into her mouth and then bolted for the bathroom. In the shower she remembered Dante and wondered if he was planning to see her today but then decided that since he knew her mother was freaky about storms and the storm was still happening, he probably expected that he wouldn't see her today. At first she was afraid she wouldn't see him again but then she remembered his jacket hanging in her robe and smiled to herself. He had to get his jacket back and he'd promised he'd see her again and kiss her again.

She thought of how he called her a beautiful witch and told her she'd bewitched him and a tingle rushed through her. He liked her lots and she knew it. Lari had called Ebony last night to tell her all about kissing Dante and she'd been thrilled for her. Ebony had a new boyfriend too – Mark, Brandon's best mate from the skating rink. And Sera had been going out with Brandon's other mate, Peter, most of the year. They were double dating to the movies this weekend and Ebony promised to ring her tomorrow night to tell her all about it. Lari was hoping to see Dante again before then so she'd have more to share as well.

Quickly Lari dressed in jeans, a t-shirt, a hoodie, and a pair of runners. She made up her face in her usual almost gothic bare minimum style and left her hair loose. Finished, she wandered back into the kitchen. "Ready, Mum."

"Great. Brad just needs to brush his teeth and we can go."

"No breakfast for him?"

"He ate while you were in the shower."

"Oh, okay," Lari could never believe how fast her younger brother could eat. On cue, he appeared behind her.

"Ready. Are we going now?" he asked.

"Yup. In the car, kids. Your dad's already there." Their mother grabbed her shoulder bag and followed them out the front door. The car was idling in the drive, their father behind the wheel. Quickly they ran through the rain and jumped into the backseat. As soon as Deb got in the car, Steve drove off, heading north to the miles of car yards.

A short hour later, they were there. The rain had eased to a drizzle and Lari and her mother hopped out when her father pulled up in front of a huge used car lot. Lari pulled the hoodie up over her head in an effort to get less wet.

"Call me if you need anything, Deb. Good luck." Deb leaned in the car window and kissed Steve goodbye.

"Thanks, honey. See you at home this afternoon. Have fun boys."

Deb and Lari waved at the car as they drove off, then her mother turned to Lari, "So, ready to look at cars?"

"Yeah," Lari looked at the sea of vehicles in all shapes and sizes. "Any idea what kind we're supposed to be looking at?"

"Okay. We have a budget of $10,000 and I'd prefer something small and with a hatch."

"Cool." Lari looked around. Lots of cars seemed to fit into that description. She wandered over to a small green two-door car with a hatch. "How about this one?" she asked. "It says $5,999 and it looks okay."

Her mother came over for a better look. "I think I might prefer four doors since I usually have to take you and Brad places. And a bit newer would be nice."

"Okay," answered Lari, moving off to look at more cars.

They looked at lots of cars, taking a few for test drives until her mother settled on a metallic blue Hyundai Accent. The salesman called it a five-door hatch, it was just under her budget and came with six month's registration. And it was only two years old.

Her mother went into the office with the salesman to finalize the paperwork while Lari kept wandering around the car yard thinking about Dante. The storm didn't seem to be happening on the north side of Adelaide and she wondered if it had stopped thundering in Christies Beach. Maybe she could spend the afternoon with Dante if it had.

She wondered if she should go to his place and knock or if that would be rude. Lari's only experience with boys before Dante was that one night kissing Brandon a week before they moved to South Australia. She wondered if there were different rules for flirting with boys here or if the rules stayed the same. In any case, she didn't want to seem desperate so she decided against going to his place uninvited.

Since her mother had voiced her concern over Dante's age, and Dante had told her he was nineteen, Lari also decided to avoid telling her mother about Dante just yet. Somehow, Lari felt her mother would think nineteen was too old and Lari didn't want to be forbidden to see Dante since she knew she'd see him anyway.

Her mother came out of the office, waving a set of keys and interrupting Lari's thoughts. "Ready to take our new car home, Lari?" her mother asked with a smile.

"Sure," Lari smiled back at her, climbing into the passenger seat.

Her mother got into the driver's seat and drove out of the car yard. Lari leaned over and turned the stereo on, flicking through the channels till she found a radio station she liked. The car was quiet and smooth and her mother looked thrilled with her purchase.

"Thanks for your help today, Lari. Want to stop and buy some lunch on our way home?"

"Yeah, okay. Where?" Lari replied.

"Oh, how about here?" her mother pointed at a Subway restaurant on the other side of the road.

"Yeah, that's cool," answered Lari. Her mother drove a bit further on till she found a break in the island and made a u-turn, doubling back to the Subway and pulling into the carpark. They got out and went in to order.

Lari chose a vegetarian six-inch on Parmesan bread and her mother went for her favourite tuna melt on wholewheat. They bought drinks and cookies to go with their rolls and sat at a table to eat.

"So, Lari. You've been surfing a lot since we got here. Made any new friends?" her mother asked.

Lari chewed and thought about her answer, remembering her decision to not talk about Dante yet. "I met some girls from school the other day."

"Shouldn't they have been in school?" her mother asked.

"Uh, it was after school ended."

"Oh, okay," her mother bought the lie and Lari was relieved.

"They said they'd show me around on Monday when I start at school."

"That will be nice. What's their names?"

"Melanie and Lisa."

"Well, I'm glad you'll know some girls. It won't be quite so daunting with some friends to show you around."

"Yeah, Mum."

"Speaking of school. I'll take you in on Monday and get you all signed in and then I'll take Brad to his school. Yours starts at eight-thirty and his starts at nine. You're okay with me not hanging around?"

"Of course, Mum. Please don't hang around. It's not cool in high school, y'know," Lari added by way of explanation.

Her mother chuckled, "Okay. I just didn't want you to think I was ditching you."

"I know you're not."

"Good. And do you want me to pick you up when school ends or will you walk home? It's straight down Beach Road, bit of a walk but mostly downhill." Her mother smiled.

"Uh, I think I can walk home. I could always phone if I change my mind."

"Okay, sounds good." Both her mother and Lari had finished eating and screwed up their wrappers. "Done?" Lari nodded. "Well, let's get home then. Thanks for your help today, Lari. If the storm's over back home you can go down the beach, if you'd like."

"Yeah, that'd be great, Mum." Lari couldn't believe her luck. Just to be safe, she mentally chanted for the storm to be gone when they got home.

FIFTEEN

The storm had faded away to nothing more than drizzle by the time they got home. Steve and Brad checked out the new car and demanded to go for a drive in it.

"I'm gonna head for the beach since the storm's gone now," she told everyone.

"Don't you want to come for a drive with us, Lari?" asked her dad.

"Hey, I've already been in it. And Mum said I could go to the beach if the storm had gone and it has."

"Yes, I did, Steve. Come on, we'll go for a drive and Lari will take her phone with her and promise to come home if the storm picks up again. Won't you, Lari?" her mother backed her up.

"All right then," her dad caved in. "Be good, Lari. We'll be home soon and you make sure you're home before dark."

"No worries." Lari went inside to change and get her board while they piled into the new car and drove off, her mother behind the wheel.

She thought about wearing Dante's jacket and decided there would be too much explaining if her parents noticed it and she was still wearing it when she came home. Then she thought about stuffing it into her bag but it didn't fit, so she decided to leave it hanging in her robe and keep the excuse that she'd have to see him again to return it.

She put on her black one-piece and then layered her t-shirt, jeans and hoodie back on over the top. Lastly, she pulled her runners back onto her feet. Her board was in its bag, ready to be carted to the beach and she almost sprinted there, she was so anxious to find out if Dante was around.

She could see that the sea was too choppy for surfing when she arrived at the beach. No-one else was there. She parked her board in the sand and sat on her towel beside it. The sand was still damp and she didn't want a wet bum in her jeans.

She was staring out into space and half-dreaming of Dante when his voice startled her out of her reverie. "Hey, Lari."

"Dante!" she exclaimed. "I didn't see you."

"No, you looked like your mind was far away. What were you thinking?"

"Why?" she cautiously answered.

"You looked like whatever it was made you very happy."

"Oh,' she paused to think for a second. "I was thinking about you."

"Oh," he answered, sitting beside her.

"Hey, do you want me to stretch out my towel? The sand's kinda wet and your butt will get wet too, if you keep sitting on the sand, that is."

"Thanks," he told her and they both got up and laid out the towel, sitting close together on it once it was rearranged.

"So, what made you come to the beach today?"

"I saw you sitting there."

"You saw me?"

"Yeah. From the house. I was upstairs on the deck, looking out over the beach and I saw you walk down and sit here."

"Oh, could you see me from that far away?" She looked over toward the house, trying to judge the distance and remember what she saw yesterday.

"Well, I worked out it was you," he amended.

She stopped trying to guess the distance and looked at his face. He was staring into her eyes and she forgot to breathe. "I left your jacket at home. I didn't know if I'd see you." She thought about how her family was out and would be gone for at least an hour or two. "We could go and get it if you want. I only live two streets away."

"Sure. You could drop your surfboard home, too. It's not really any good for surfing out there." He waved his hand toward the water as he spoke.

"No, it's not." They got up and she threw her sandy towel over her shoulder. Dante picked up her board and carried it for her. They started walking up the road towards her home.

"Would you like to go for a drive with me? Do some of that sightseeing?" he asked as they walked.

"Yeah, sure! Do you drive?" she asked.

"Of course."

"Well, I've never seen you in a car."

"No, I don't think they'd like me driving on the beach."

"Haha. Very funny." They arrived at her house and Lari was relieved to see that her family was still out. She dropped her surfboard off and got Dante's jacket from her robe while he waited in the family room.

"Thanks," he told her, taking his jacket. "Do you need to leave a note or anything?"

"No," she stopped and thought for a minute. "Okay, maybe." She grabbed a sticky note and scrawled, 'No good for surfing, hanging with new friends. Home before dark. Got my phone. Love Lari.'

"Hanging with friends?" he laughed. "So I'm plural, huh?"

"Don't be rude. You shouldn't be reading other people's letters."

"Letters? That's a bit of a stretch." She grabbed his hand and pulled him out the door. As they left he frowned, "You haven't told them about me, have you?"

"Oh, kinda. Can we not talk about this right now?"

"Okay." He sounded doubtful, but changed the conversation. "Where would you like to go?"

"I dunno. Show me somewhere you like. I still have to be home before dark, though, so not too far away, I guess."

"Okay." They were at his house in no time and he walked her to the big triple garage that was part of the building.

"Oh, monster garage!" she gasped as he pushed a remote and one of the doors lifted to reveal a brand new metallic black 370Z sports car parked beside a new looking pearl grey Mercedes and a yellow RX8. "Is that yours?" she squealed when he opened the passenger door to the 370Z, and when he smiled and nodded, she squealed again, "That is just... just... awesome!"

She jumped in the passenger seat and Dante climbed into the driver's side, starting the engine almost immediately. The throaty roar of the motor was almost instantly drowned out by the sound of Muse blaring from the speakers. He quickly lowered the volume with the remote and Lari looked at him, gaping.

"This is fucking amazing."

His eyes widened.

"I'm sorry," she said, realizing she'd only ever used baby swear words around him. "I didn't mean to swear." Lari tried to look apologetic and only succeeded in looking like she was trying not to laugh.

He grinned, "You should be! Such language from a pretty young thing like you!" He laughed and she did too.

"Smart arse." She was silent as they backed out of the garage and turned around in the drive. "This house is just amazing and so is your car."

He didn't answer. Instead he pushed a button on a remote and a set of gates slid open to reveal the road. He drove slowly through Port Noarlunga turning off after he crossed the Onkaparinga River to take the Esplanade along the beach where he gunned the engine and drove so fast the car almost flew, braking hard for every roundabout and slow-down point.

Lari resisted the urge to swear again, figuring he didn't like it much, and instead she dug her fingers into the seat, her knuckles turning white.

"You could go a little bit slower, maybe," she volunteered through gritted teeth as the scenery outside the car blurred.

He turned to look at her frightened face and slowed down almost immediately. "Sorry. Didn't mean to scare you. I love going fast in this car. Just a habit, I guess."

"You call that fast? I call it light speed," she joked now that they'd slowed to a more reasonable speed.

"Oh, funny!" he laughed with her.

She realized they were heading south along the coast. "So, where are we going?"

"Down to Cape Jervois. There's this great little bay there that I wanted to show you. I thought I'd show you one of my favourite places. It's faster to go via Main South Road but I thought you'd like to see as much of the coastline as you could. We'll end up back on Main South Road eventually and we can go home that way."

"Yeah. Sounds good." She looked out the window. "Actually, scenery's pretty good now we're going slow enough that I can see it."

"You're never gonna let that go, are you?" he asked with a smile.

"Oh, not for a little while. Planes go that fast, not cars."

He shook his head and laughed. "My beautiful little coward."

Lari was about to tell him off for calling her a coward when she realized he said she was his. She opened her mouth and closed it again.

"You were going to say something?" he asked.

"Nope," she answered. "Just watching the view. At normal speed."

He grinned and so did she. The coastline whizzed by and a little over an hour after they left his house, he pulled off into a cliff-side car park. "We're almost there," he told her.

"Wow! What a view!" she exclaimed looking out over the expanse of blue.

"I wanted you to see the view first but we'll drive down there so I can take you to the place I told you about." He pointed to a bare expanse of rocky ground by the foreshore below them. "Then there's a little bit of a walk." Quickly he pulled out again and drove down to the foreshore, driving slowly over the rough ground and parking the car close to the edge.

SIXTEEN

His idea of a little bit of a walk turned out to be a hike down uneven rocky ground that a mountain goat would've loved, but Lari didn't mind too much since it gave her plenty of excuses to grab hold of him.

They clambered down and hiked along the shore out of sight, stopping in a sheltered bay where a small cave-like alcove that wasn't visible from the top was carved into the rock by years of weathering. They sat just inside the alcove, protected from the elements and looked out over the rough water.

"It is beautiful," she told him. "Do you come here much?"

"As often as I can," he answered, draping an arm around her shoulders. She snuggled into him, smiling widely. He felt cold and she wondered why he didn't dress more warmly since he always seemed to be cold.

"How come you always feel so cold?" she asked. "Seriously, you radiate cold."

He sighed. "We need to talk, only I'm not sure how to go about this."

Larissa frowned. This sounded like a break-up speech was coming; only they weren't even properly going out yet. "Why? Because I asked why you're always so cold?" She paused. "Are you trying to break up with me or something coz I thought we had to be going out first?" Then she had another thought. "Are you sick or something?"

"Huh? Oh, no. I don't think so. I just have something really important to tell you and I don't know how to say it. I've never had to do this before."

"Oh." Larissa was stumped, wondering what was so hard to tell her. "Do you have a girlfriend?"

"No."

"Oh." Her mind went blank.

"I don't have a girlfriend, and I don't know if you'd describe... I'm not sick, or at least, I don't think I am, and I don't want to stop seeing you but you might want to stop seeing me after I tell you what I have to."

"Tell away before I go crazy trying to guess." Larissa stared out to sea. Her throat felt as choked as the day she left Sydney.

Dante reached over and held her hand. "I promise I'm not trying to end things with you. I'm crazy about you. I tried to not see you but I couldn't do it."

Lari looked over at him. "Really?" She could feel her throat relaxing.

"Yes. When you bumped into me at the library, I really was bewitched by you. Then I saw you again at the beach and I had to talk to you. After I found out you were only fifteen, I told myself I had to stay away from you, but I just couldn't do it."

60

"Nearly sixteen and none of this sounds bad."

"I know," he sighed. "I haven't told you the big stuff yet."

"Well, tell me."

He sighed again. "Do you believe in love at first sight?"

"Yes." Lari didn't hesitate. She was crazy about Dante and yet they'd only just met.

"Me too." He stared out to sea. "I think... I want to be with you. Being with you means I have to share stuff I've never shared with... anyone else before." He paused again. "This is so hard." He glanced across at her. She was staring out to sea, her face tense. "You asked me how come I'm always cold. What I have to say is related to that." He paused and kept looking out over the water. "I told you I don't feel the cold, and I don't. But my skin does always feel cold. Well, most of the time it feels cold to touch."

She looked at him. "Are you gonna tell me why?"

"Yes," he paused and swallowed. "I really don't know how to say this," he muttered. The pause went on for ages and finally he blurted, "I'm... I'm a vampire, Lari. The living dead." He glanced across at her. She was looking at him, open-mouthed. "I died in 1887 in Whitby and I woke up a day later as a vampire. I've been nineteen ever since then." He looked at her again.

Lari was still silent, her eyes huge and staring, fixed on him.

"Please say something," he pleaded in a worried voice.

Lari swallowed, closed her mouth, opened it again, closed it once more, and finally spoke, "A vampire? Vampires aren't real. Are they?"

"They're real, Lari. I'm real."

"Prove it," she told him. "Hang on. How will you prove it? Do you suck blood? Kill people? You don't have fangs. At least, I haven't noticed any fangs. And you go out in daytime and sun and stuff. I'm babbling."

He waited till she stopped speaking. "Yes, I do drink blood but I try not to kill people. And I do have fangs; they're just not as big as people think they'll be. They are very sharp. Sharp enough to do their job. I can go out in daytime and sunlight coz it's just a myth that vampires can't but I don't spend too much time in the sun or people would wonder why I don't tan. And garlic and crosses and a whole bunch of other stuff are just myths, too."

"So you don't turn to ashes or burn or... or sparkle... or... or...."

"No," he smiled softly. "I just don't tan at all. My skin never changes colour."

"You look normal. Except that you're so pale."

"Of course. If I looked vastly different, how would I blend into normal society? My ability to survive depends on me being able to blend in. And I was pale even when I was alive."

61

"Oh," she paused. Then, her eyes wide, she continued, "Do you suck animal blood then? Instead of people?"

"No," he shuddered. "Somehow that just seems gross."

"That seems gross?" Lari was astonished. "If you suck people's blood and you don't kill them, how do you do it? I mean, how come people don't say anything about it?"

"It's a sort of mind control, kind of like hypnosis. I tell them they won't remember it and most of the time they don't. All they remember is having some kind of pleasurable dream. And my fang marks fade before they wake. It doesn't work on some people, but mostly it does."

"1887?" she asked. "That makes you..." she started doing the math in her head.

"One hundred and twenty years ago and I was nineteen when it happened."

"Oh," she paused. "Have you sucked my blood?"

"No."

"Would you tell me if you did?

"Yes."

"Would you suck my blood?"

"No."

"Why not?"

"I don't want to think of you like that."

"Like what?"

"Food."

"Oh," she paused. "You said the people whose blood you sucked get pleasure from it. Don't you too?"

"Kind of."

"Don't you want to..." she didn't know how to finish the sentence.

"Lari, you haven't run away or let go of my hand," he said softly, staring into her eyes.

"No. I don't want to," she stared back at him. "You won't hurt me, will you?"

"No. I don't ever want to hurt you."

"Then kiss me."

He stared deeply into her eyes and then gently kissed her. She pulled her hand out of his and wrapped her arms around his neck, drawing him to her. The kiss was deeper and more passionate than their first and then he was pulling away and she was breathing heavy.

"Oh, Dante. I want to be with you."

"Larissa," the way he said her name made it sound sexy and beautiful. "I want to be with you too."

"The way you say Larissa makes it sound beautiful." She was still breathing heavy and staring into his eyes. "Are we a real couple now?"

"Yes." He kissed her lightly again. "Thank you."

"For what?"

"Not running away. Wanting me."

"I couldn't imagine running away from you. You're perfect. Even if you are a vampire." She chuckled softly. "I think maybe I need more time to process that last bit, but I still won't run away from you."

He smiled back at her. "If you don't want us to drive at light speed as you called it, we better start heading back so you can be home before dark."

"Okay." She grinned and continued, "Hey, can you do anything special, like super powers or stuff?"

"Maybe," he grinned back at her. "I told you about the mind control already. I'm super strong, I have exceptional eyesight, I'm incredibly coordinated and I can run extremely fast and coz I don't need to breathe, I can swim underwater for a really long time."

Lari was distracted, her mind still trying to comprehend that Dante was a vampire and that vampires were real, so she wasn't fully listening to him. "That's cool," she answered flippantly. They started climbing back up the rocky route to the car and Lari was struggling to keep her grip. A third of the way back, she stopped and looked at him with a slight frown.

"What?"

"You haven't used that mind control thing on me, have you?"

"No," he laughed. "I wouldn't." He held out his hand. "Want me to carry you?" he smiled. "I can carry you and we'll climb really fast."

"You won't fall?"

"No."

"Then carry me please!" He lifted her onto his back and started racing up the cliffs. They were at the top and next to his car in a little over three minutes. "Wow! That was great! I liked that." He let her drop to the ground and she whirled to hug him. It was like hugging a cold rock that could wrap its arms around her. He kissed her gently.

"You like me running really fast with you on my back, but not driving fast?"

"Yes, it's different."

He laughed and shook his head. "Okay, my beautiful witch. It's time to get you home."

She jumped into the passenger seat and he gunned the engine, driving back toward her home. "You better drop me down the road from my place. Pick

63

me up at my place tomorrow lunchtime and I'll introduce you to my 'rents then. Is that okay?" she told him as they neared her house.

"Do you want me to walk or drive to your place tomorrow?"

"Walk. No, drive. Then we can go back to that cave again. I want to talk more with you. I have questions." She reached over and brushed his cheek with her hand. "I want to kiss you more, too," she added.

"Are you going to tell them you were out with me today?"

"I don't know yet. Don't push it. They're gonna think you're a bit old for me at nineteen. Imagine how they'd carry on if they knew you were actually one hundred and thirty-nine years old!" she laughed and leaned on his shoulder.

He pulled up just around the corner from her house. "See you tomorrow, Lari," he said, staring into her eyes. "I can't believe you're not calling me a freak and running away from me."

"No way. Seriously, are you telling me only freaks and weirdos would wanna be with me?" she asked him jokingly. Dante shook his head, smiling at her and Lari continued, "Smart man, right answer! Now kiss me goodbye and promise to see me at lunchtime tomorrow."

He obligingly leaned over to kiss her and whispered his promise to see her at noon. Larissa felt a thrill of pleasure throughout her body and sighed, smiling as she stepped out of the car, waving to him as he drove away.

She walked round the corner and into her house. Everyone was home. She needed time alone to process everything and figure out how to tell them she had a boyfriend and he was coming over to pick her up tomorrow. Meantime, she'd have to smile and be normal so they'd leave her alone later in the evening.

SEVENTEEN

Her mother was making dinner as she walked in the door. Lari called out that she was home and went straight to her room. She turned on her iPod and sprawled on her bed to think about the day's events.

Dante was a hundred and thirty-nine year old vampire. Her head couldn't quite get around that idea but she'd been on his back when he ran up the rocky shore that had taken them nearly ten minutes to clamber down. And he did always feel cold to touch. She knew she was going to have plenty more questions for him tomorrow.

A little thrill of excitement washed over her as she remembered that he was her boyfriend and that he'd said he was crazy about her. He'd asked her if she believed in love at first sight. She was almost sure that he'd nearly told her he loved her. Her vampire boyfriend. Then she realized she'd have to tell her parents somehow and before he came to pick her up tomorrow, though she knew she'd leave out the part about him being a vampire.

A stabbing pain in her head made her cry out, "Ouch. Oh not one of those stupid headaches now," she groaned. Ever since she reached puberty she'd been getting terrible headaches. Sometimes they lasted hours and other times they were gone as fast as they appeared.

She slowly got off the bed to avoid making her head throb too much and walked out to the laundry where the medicine cabinet was. The laundry was past the kitchen so she had to walk past her mother, who was standing over the stove, cooking.

"You all right, Lari? You look a little pale."

"Headache," she said softly, trying to avoid making it worse.

"Oh, that's two in one day. Maybe it's the weather," her mother replied. "Go lay down for half an hour. I'm trying out a new recipe and it'll be about that long before dinner's ready."

"Ta, Mum," she answered, pulling the packet of Panadol Rapid from the cabinet and grabbing two of the tablets, dropped them into a glass of water. She watched them fizz and dissolve and then drank it quickly.

Relieved to be saved from a conversation she wasn't ready for, she headed back to her room and lay down on her bed again. She closed her eyes and thought about Dante.

She woke a little while later to her mother gently shaking her. "Lari, wake up, honey," her mother was saying.

"Mmmmn, awake, Mum," she mumbled.

"Dinner's ready. Are you feeling better?"

65

"Yeah, I think so," she answered as she sat up and realized her headache appeared to have gone.

"Good. Come have dinner." Her mother left the room and Lari got up and followed her out.

Dinner was a seafood dish that had turned out quite well. Her mother was pleased that they all liked it and she'd even made an apple pie for dessert.

While her mother served the apple pie, her dad asked, "So, Lari, where'd you go this afternoon? Thanks for the note, too."

"For a drive down to Cape Jervois. Some sightseeing."

"A drive? Who drove?"

"It was Dante. You remember I told you about him. He was at the beach today too."

"Dante? Have I heard about him?" he looked at her mother.

"I have, Steve. He's a boy Lari met at the library the day we got here and I think they've met down the beach a few times too." Her mother looked pointedly at Lari, as if to tell her that she knew Lari had been meeting him at the beach, even if Lari hadn't been forthcoming about that.

"Yeah, they made googly eyes at each other at the beach when I was there!" Brad interjected.

"Shut up, Brad!" hissed Lari. "We did not!"

"Oh," her father continued, ignoring Brad's outburst. "You went for a drive with him? He has a car?" Her father sounded a little unhappy about events but he hadn't told her off yet.

"Yeah. The waves were crap so he offered to take me sightseeing down the coast. We just drove down to Cape Jervois and back. Wait till you see his car! It's so cool."

"How old is this boy?" her father asked and her mother looked at her as well.

It was crunch time. Lari thought about lying but decided that it wasn't the smart thing to do since they'd meet him tomorrow and probably ask him a million questions. "He's nineteen." She glanced at her mother, "I asked after Mum wanted to know."

"Nineteen? He's a little older than you thought he was, and a little old for you, isn't he?" asked her mother.

"No, he's not too old. I'm sixteen in a couple of months and it's only like three years," Lari was firm. She remembered that he was actually one hundred and thirty-nine if you counted all the years since he became a vampire but she didn't think her parents would handle that information very well. "I like him a lot and he likes me and he's going to pick me up tomorrow at lunchtime so he can meet you."

66

Her mother sighed and looked like she wanted to say something different to what she actually said. "Well, I'm glad we're going to meet this boy and I think you've been seeing him more than you've let on, Lari."

"Not really. We never made any dates or anything." It was a little white lie but she figured it didn't matter if it helped them get used to the idea of Dante.

"What does this nineteen year old Dante do when he's not romancing my daughter, then?" asked her father.

"Dad! He's at uni studying philosophy."

"Philosophy? What does someone who studies that do when they leave uni?"

"I dunno. You can ask him tomorrow."

"And where's he planning to take you tomorrow then?"

"More sightseeing. He thinks I'm lame for spending all last week at the beach and not looking around."

"He does have a point there. Though, as you can't drive and your mother only got a car today, it would've been a bit difficult for you to actually do any sightseeing."

"Okay, so is this conversation over now? I wanna go watch a movie."

"All right. Go. Watch your movie," her mother told her as she began clearing the table.

Brad immediately ran for the living room. "I'm watching something in here!" he called out, beating her there.

"Fine." Lari was glad Brad had beaten her to the living room as she much preferred to hang out in her own room and the movie was just an excuse to end the conversation and leave the table. She had her own TV and DVD player so her parents wouldn't question why she didn't put up a fight over the living room.

EIGHTEEN

It seemed to take forever to get to noon. Larissa was showered and dressed before nine and spent the next three hours anxiously waiting for Dante to arrive.

She heard his car before she saw it. Remembering how fast he liked to drive, she crossed her fingers that he'd drive up at a saner speed.

It was as if he could hear her thoughts. His car crawled along the street at a slow thirty or forty kilometres an hour. He parked in front of their house.

"He's here!" she called out.

Her mother walked over to the window and looked out. "Oh, that is a nice looking car. Looks expensive." She turned to Lari. "Does his family have money? You never mentioned it."

"Yeah. Probably. He lives in that house on top of the cliff by the beach. I told you. The one with the big fence and all the glass and stuff. You can see pretty much all of Christies Beach from there. He said they call the area Witton Bluff."

"Oh." Her mother blinked a few times and then looked back out the window in time to see Dante walking in the gate. "And he is attractive, isn't he?" she said softly.

Her father joined them at the window. "That's a new 370Z. Very nice car. Can't imagine a lot of nineteen year old uni students can afford one of those."

Just then the doorbell rang. "I'll get it!" Lari called as she ran for the door, opening it immediately. "Hi," she greeted him.

"Hi," he answered.

"They're waiting for you in the living room." She smiled at him and whispered, "I think they're gonna let me go out with you without a fight!"

"Good," he whispered back. "I won't have to use any super powers then." He grinned and winked at her, following her into the living room where her parents were now seated. "Hi, I'm Dante," he greeted them with a smile.

"Hello Dante," both her parents chorused.

"Nice to meet you," her mother added.

"You too," he replied.

"I'm Steve Parker and this is my wife, Lari's mother, Deb. Have a seat," her father told him. "Would you like something to drink, Dante? Tea, coffee, soft drink, juice? I won't offer you alcohol when you're planning to take my daughter for a drive."

"No, nothing for me, thanks, and I don't drink alcohol." Dante sat in one of the theatre chairs. "These are pretty good," he told her parents. "Nice set up."

Her father smiled. "Yeah, I set it up myself. You don't drink alcohol? Good for you." Her father seemed to relax a little. "So, Dante, Lari tells me you're studying philosophy at uni, and is that an English accent you have there?"

"Ah, yes. Studying philosophy at Uni SA and yes, I'm from England."

"Hmmmn. What will you do once you've finished with uni?"

"I have another year of this degree and then I'm thinking of doing some post-grad study so I won't be finished with uni for a while yet."

"Oh, okay." Her father didn't seem to be questioning Dante as much as Lari had expected. "Is that a new 370Z you're driving?"

"Yes. It's about six months old now, I guess."

"Nice car."

"Thanks." He smiled.

"Where are you planning to go today?"

"I thought I'd drive north and show her some of the Barossa Valley and then head back this way and show her more of the Fleurieu Peninsula, maybe out through McLaren Vale and Clarendon, and then probably down the coast to Cape Jervois since Lari liked Cape Jervois so much yesterday. If we have enough time for all of that."

"Okay," Steve turned to Lari. "You have your phone?" She nodded and he continued, "So, I guess you two want to head out," he said, still looking at Lari who was sitting nervously at the edge of the ottoman. Again she nodded. He turned back to Dante. "A few things before you go, Dante." Her father's voice took on a serious tone. "Larissa is still only fifteen, despite her repeated insistence that she's nearly sixteen, and I'd appreciate it if you'd remember that. Don't do anything stupid in that car while my daughter is in it, and take good care of her. Also, she normally has to be home by dark. However, her mother and I have decided to make an exception tonight and ask that you please bring her home before nine o'clock. She starts school tomorrow so we'd prefer she not be out too late."

"Oh thanks!" Lari leaped off the ottoman and hugged each of her parents.

"Thank you," added Dante. "I promise to take excellent care of her and she'll be home before nine and safe." He stood and looked at Lari. "Are you ready?"

"Yes, I'll just grab my bag and phone." She ran out of the room and returned a minute later with her messenger bag slung over her shoulder. "Bye Mum, bye Dad! See ya tonight!"

"Have fun and be safe!" her mother called out.

"Bye sweetie," her father said. "Remember what I told you, Dante, and we'll be fine."

"No problems, Mr Parker."

Larissa grabbed Dante's hand as they walked down the path and out the gate to his car. She was so excited and happy and her parents had not only allowed her to go out with Dante, they'd approved her staying out with him until nine o'clock.

"Are we really going to all those places before we head to Cape Jervois like you told my 'rents?" she asked as they drove off.

"Yes. I thought we could drive and you could see the sights and you can still ply me with questions if you have them."

"I have tons," she smiled. "But I can't really kiss you while you're driving and I want to do that too."

He laughed. "We can do that when we stop."

"Awesome," she grinned and leaned over to rest her head against his shoulder.

"So, the questions?" he prompted.

"All right... Can you eat or drink anything except blood?"

"Yes. But it tastes terrible and I'd rather not."

"How do you avoid eating and drinking around people without them ever noticing?"

"I'm not usually around people long enough for them to notice I don't eat like them."

"You're around people all the time... Well, lots of the time."

"Yes. But I don't spend the whole day with them. And if mealtimes happen when I'm with someone I usually just say I'm on some weird diet. Or if I'm somewhere I can order something like steak tartare, I'll do that. It's not quite so bad tasting, but still pretty terrible for me."

"Oh yeah. Like you did that day at the beach with me." Then she realized what he'd said he'd eat. "Steak tartare? Isn't that raw meat?"

"Yes."

"Ewwwww!" She pulled a face. "Yuk, yuk, yuk!" Then she remembered something else she wanted to know and her expression changed. "Oooh! How about the cold thing? You said your skin felt cold most of the time. Explain that to me."

"Okay. Nearly all the time, my skin feels cold. But if it's a really hot day and I'm out in the sun for most of it, my skin will feel warmer to touch, kind of like a reptile."

70

"That's cool."

"You think?" he looked startled.

"Yeah. I do." Without skipping a beat, she continued, "Can we have sex?"

"What?" He looked stunned. "Are you asking for sex or if it's physically possible?"

"Ummnn... Can you look at the road again?" He returned to watching the road as he drove and she tilted her head as she thought about his question. "Well, I was just asking if it was physically possible, but y'know, the other sounds okay too."

"Cheeky!" he told her. "Physically it's possible but I'd have to be so careful not to hurt you that I don't think I'd be willing to do it. At least not until I was really sure I wouldn't break you."

"Could I get pregnant? Like would I still need contraceptives or stuff?"

"No."

"But what about the stories about incubus and stuff? Did I say that right?"

"Close enough. Those are stories to do with demons and not vampires."

"Are they real too?"

"Maybe. I'm not a hundred percent sure. I haven't come across any but that doesn't mean they aren't real."

She changed direction again, "How come you don't wanna suck my blood?"

"I told you. Blood is food for me and I don't want to think of you that way. I don't think of you that way."

"But you said you get pleasure from it too."

"Yes, that's true." He paused, then asked, "Do you want me to drink from you? Is that why you're asking?"

"I dunno. I think I kinda want you to want to but I don't know if I actually want you to. Did that make sense?"

He chuckled. "Yeah, kind of. I think I understood it, anyway."

NINETEEN

They reached the Barossa Valley a couple of hours later. He parked the car and removed a picnic basket from the backseat.

"A picnic basket? You don't eat!" she exclaimed.

Dante replied, "But you do. It's for you."

"Oh, you're just so cool!" Larissa hugged him. "What did ya get me?"

"Wait and see," he grinned, pleased that she was impressed. "Walk this way, beautiful."

She took his free hand and walked up the hillside with him. It was a gentle climb and they reached the top in a few minutes. The view was extraordinary. She could see hills and valleys and fields of grapevines dotted around clusters of housing estates.

"Oh, wow! You know the most amazing places!"

"Thank you." He pulled a rug from the top of the picnic basket and laid it on the grassy slope.

They sat down next to each other and she immediately dived into the basket. Pulling her hands out, she looked at him, worried for a moment. "There's no raw meat in here, is there?"

"No," he smiled.

She went back to rummaging in around the thermal cooling blocks to find the food.

"Oh, cool! You have cans of drink and how did you know I don't eat meat? There's only seafood and salad stuff here!"

"I didn't. I've only ever seen you eat seafood so I knew you liked that and I just put in the salads coz I thought you might eat them."

"You're brilliant!" She flung herself at him, hugging and kissing him. "I'm not hungry yet but I am thirsty," she said grabbing a can of drink and closing the lid on the basket. She cracked open the can and drank half of it.

"So, are you done with the questions or do you have more for me?"

"I think I'm done with vampire questions for now. But I might have more later." She grinned at him. "I have a vampire boyfriend." She giggled. "I'm sorry, it just sounds so strange."

He smiled at her. "I have a human girlfriend. It is strange."

"Oh!" her eyes opened wide. "Call me strange, will you!" She lightly thumped him. "So not fair! Hitting you is like hitting a rock."

He laughed and leaned in to kiss her. "Would you rather we did this?" he asked, kissing her some more.

"Oooh, yes. More of that please," she whispered, laying down, pulling him with her and kissing him back.

She tightened her grip on him, drawing him closer to her, twining her legs around him as they kissed more passionately. There was nothing soft about him; he was a smooth, hard, cool rock that moved.

He broke away from kissing her, "Are you trying to take me prisoner?" he asked, his voice husky.

"Forever," she answered, her voice just as throaty, her eyes glazed with lust.

"Beautiful girl," he said, staring into her eyes. "Break time." He pulled free of her grip and rolled over to lie next to her.

"Ohhhh..." she frowned, rolling onto her side to pout at him.

He laughed gently. "Pouting? You're exquisite. Now stop it." His voice sounded more normal.

She pouted more, and then unable to keep it up, settled for snuggling next to him.

His fingers threaded through her hair. "I like your hair hanging loose like this," he told her. "Like a beautiful silky gold curtain of curls."

She twisted to face him, twining her fingers through his dark locks, "Yours is the silkiest hair I've ever felt. It looks so silky and feels even better." She felt his lips brush the top of her head. "Dante, tell me about how you became a vampire."

He was incredibly still for a minute, and then he started talking. "It was 1887 and I was in Whitby. Do you know where Whitby is?"

"Yeah. My great-grandparents are from Whitby."

"Really? Great-grandparents? When did they live there?" He sounded slightly excited.

"It was sometime in the mid to late nineteen twenties I think. My grandpa was born in Australia in 1936 and my great grandma was twenty when he was born."

"Oh," he sounded disappointed. Then he smiled, "So your great-great-great grandparents would've lived in Whitby when I did?"

"Probably... how many greats was that?"

"Three. Do you know what their name was?"

"Ummn... they're my grandparents on Mum's side so their last name would've been Williams."

"Williams? I knew a James Williams when I was alive. He was the same age as me. He was betrothed to Fanny Taylor."

"Oh my God! There's a James and Fanny Williams in our family. I remember coz I've always laughed at her name. Fanny's a really strange

73

name for nowadays and I don't know about England, but here in Australia that's also a female body part."

Dante shook his head, smiling. "They must be the same people. I grew up with your great-great-great grandfather. That's a bit of a shock."

"It is pretty freaky. Maybe it's fate that we're together now."

"Maybe." He paused and looked at her. "You have a somewhat quirky way of looking at things sometimes."

"Yeah, that's probably helpful when dating a vampire."

He laughed. "What's that phrase you like so much?" He thought for a second, "Oh yeah... smart arse!" He kissed her lightly.

"So, come on. You were telling me about becoming a vampire," she urged him.

"Okay. I was in Whitby and it was 1887 and I'd just turned nineteen. James and I had been out to a tavern for a few drinks and we were celebrating my birthday and his upcoming wedding. He wanted to go straight home but I wasn't ready for sleep yet and I decided to take a walk up by the church, the one made famous by Bram Stoker. This was a good ten years before Bram Stoker's story about Dracula was published, too. It was our local parish church, where James and Fanny were to be married, nothing more. There was no reason for me to fear going there, day or night. We said goodnight at the bottom of the stairs and he went home. I walked up the stairs and strolled along the cliff edge for a while. I was standing there looking out to sea when a voice spoke from behind me.

"Are you here alone?" he asked.

His voice was raspy. "Yes," I told him. I was about to turn to see who was speaking to me when I felt him grab my shoulders and his fangs sunk into my neck. He could've hypnotized me but he didn't. Perhaps he thought that since he had the advantage anyway, he didn't need to, or perhaps he was just too thirsty. I don't know why I didn't fight him. Possibly I was too drunk or too shocked, or both.

He drank and I passed out. I woke the next day. I was in the ruined abbey just along from the church. My head hurt and I was thirsty. I couldn't see him, but he sensed I had awoken and spoke to me. His voice didn't sound so raspy now.

"You are no longer one of the living. You are the undead. A vampire like me. The raging thirst you feel is for blood. You will want to drink. You will drink a lot over the next few months and then your thirst will lessen. You will always want blood. It is your food and water. But you will age no more and you will never die. You will be incredibly strong and it will be difficult for any

74

to kill you, although it is not impossible. Avoid fire, it is your enemy. I will stay with you for these first few days and then I must leave. I'm sorry. I didn't intend to do this to you. It is not necessary to turn everyone you drink from into a vampire, nor is it necessary to kill anyone. I did this because I had not drunk for too long and my thirst was so great that I drank too deeply from you. I had to choose whether to let you die or to make you a vampire. I chose this. If you would rather have died, I am sorry. Let my mistake be a lesson to you. Do not go too long without drinking."

I didn't know what to say. I was stunned, speechless, and the thirst he described was rampaging within me.

He kept me hidden inside the abbey all day, telling me that my friends and family would believe I had fallen from the cliff in my drunken state and that I must never see them again.

That night, when it was safely dark, he took me out to feed for the first time. I learnt how to take the blood I needed without killing anyone and the next day I left with him to go to London where I lived for the next few years.

I found out very quickly that I could live among humans and not be noticed for what I was, as long as I was careful about mealtimes, mine and human, and didn't stay in one place for so many years that my lack of aging became apparent.

My creator left me a week after we arrived in London and I've never seen him since. He was a loner, I think, and truly sorry he made me." He paused, "There, that's the story."

"Wow." Larissa was quiet, thinking. "You grew up with my... how many greats was it?"

"Three."

"Great-great-great grandpa. James Williams was your friend and you were out with him the last night you were human."

"Yes." He seemed nervous.

"I wonder if I'd find anything about you if I looked up old family stuff."

"Maybe. Does your old family stuff go back that far?"

"Yeah, Mum's family is anal about family history and James is, was on her side of things."

"I'd like it if you could. I had to leave so soon after and I couldn't, didn't go back there until the early nineteen thirties. I didn't want to ask about any of my old family or friends in case I was recognized. It would be nice to know what happened to James. He got married to Fanny and had children, obviously."

75

"Yes, he clearly did that." Larissa laughed. "Really, we were meant to be together. It's fate, for sure."

"You said that before."

"Yup, I believe it totally. Hey," she said, changing tack, "did you know the name of the guy who changed you?"

"No. He never told me. Just taught me what to do and left."

"The people you live with now, are they vampires?"

"Yes.

"What's your last name, Dante?"

"Hill."

"Cool. I'll remember that for when I'm looking through our family stuff. I better not tell Mum and Dad what I'm doing coz they might think it's weird that you have the same name as James's friend... if you're mentioned in our stuff, that is."

"Thank you, Lari. You can't know how much it means to me that you're doing this."

"Did you have a girlfriend before y'know, you changed?"

"No. That was partly why I was up there walking the cliffs. I would have my fun with the local girls but I hadn't met any I wanted to marry. James getting married had me thinking about my future."

"Well, maybe you just had to get to the right century so you could meet me."

He chuckled, "Maybe." He tapped the picnic basket with his foot. "Hungry, yet?"

"Yeah, a bit." She sat up and grabbed some of the food and ate. "This is wicked. Did you make it?"

"No, bought it."

"Oh well, it's still wicked." She finished eating and opened another can, drinking half in one go again.

"You just throw them down, don't you?" he asked. She nodded and smiled. "Okay, do you want to stay here longer or head down to that rock cave at Cape Jervois?"

"Oh, the Cape, please. I loved that place."

"The Cape it is, then." He packed away the rug and the leftover food, taking her hand and carrying the basket back to the car. He unlocked it with the remote and they got inside, turning around to drive south. He paused before they started driving down the road, letting the engine idle. "Side trips through the Fleurieu or straight to the Cape?"

"Straight there. More talking and kissing." She leaned over and quickly kissed his cold cheek, giving him a flirty smile as she sat back in her seat.

TWENTY

They reached Cape Jervois and the little rocky cave just under three hours later. The sun was just starting to set. Lari stared at it, watching the sun sink below the horizon. "Look at that. Isn't it pretty?"

She shivered once as she got out of the car and Dante noticed. "Cold?" There was a slight chill to the air and Lari realized she'd forgotten to bring a hoodie with her.

"A bit. I forgot my hoodie."

"Well, lucky this is still in here, then," he told her, reaching into the back to grab the jacket she'd borrowed from him and returned yesterday.

"Yay, it's mine again!" she giggled, putting it on.

"Yeah, I don't really need jackets or stuff. I just wear them so people won't notice anything weird like me standing in freezing cold weather wearing shorts and a t-shirt."

"So, you really don't feel the cold?"

"No."

"Heat?"

"Nope. It's always the same temperature for me. Except that sometimes if I'm in the hot sun for a long time, my skin feels warmer to you."

"That spins me out."

"That does? Not that I'm a vampire or a hundred and thirty-nine or that I drink blood? It spins you out that I don't feel changes in temperature?"

"Oooh, I was gonna give you a thump and then I remembered you're a rock!"

He laughed. "Sunset's over. Want me to carry you down? It's faster and I won't fall."

"Like you carried me back yesterday?" He nodded. "Yes please! I really liked that."

The ride to the cave was even more fun as Lari could see the water over his shoulder. They got to the cave and she slid off his back, quickly jumping in front of him to plant a kiss on his lips. "Thank you, that is just so cool!"

They snuggled into the alcove, huddling next to each other. "Are you sure you're okay with dating a vampire, Lari?"

"Yup. Sucks that I can't actually tell anyone you're a vampire. I can't tell, can I?"

"I'd prefer that you didn't."

"Yeah, thought so. It's not like you advertise it or anything. But it's really not a big deal for me. Part of me thinks there's gotta be something wrong with me, mentally, y'know, coz it should be a big deal, shouldn't it?" She looked up at him, before continuing, "but it's just not a big deal for me. I can't get worked up about it. It's like you said you were from another country or something. Well, you are from another country too. I thought about it lots last night but I don't know. Maybe it's just that it doesn't seem fully real yet. I don't know. Anyway, I like you just the way you are. And there are some really cool bonuses like the carrying me thing and I can pinch your jacket anytime I'm cold and not feel guilty that you're gonna be cold. I'm rambling, aren't I?"

"It's okay. You can ramble if you want. And some of the things you called bonuses are kind of good, I guess," he smiled and draped his arm around her shoulder. She nestled in closer.

"So, Dante, the other people you live with, the other vampires... what are they like? How old are they? Do they know about me?"

"They're friends. How to describe their ages... Do you want to know the ages they were when they became vampires or how long they've been vampires?"

"Both."

"Okay. There's Kristof. He's originally from Hungary and he's been a vampire since 1586. He was twenty-five when he became a vampire. Kris is with Lucinda. She's from America and was about seventeen when she was changed. Kris met her there in the 1700s. She'd been changed by a savage vampire and left to fend for herself. She knew nothing. At least the one who changed me stuck around long enough to show me what I needed to know. Kris said Lucinda was being hunted as a wild animal because the townspeople didn't realize what she was. They thought they were hunting some wild beast that was slaughtering their sheep and unwary villagers."

"Oh, was she killing them? Animals and people?"

"Yes. She didn't know any better. Kris worked out what was happening and found her. He taught her how to feed without savagery or killing and took her away from there. They've been together ever since."

"That's romantic."

"You think?" He raised his eyebrows as he looked at her. "I say again, you have a quirky way of looking at things." He continued, "Then there's Cristóbal. He's Spanish and was eighteen in 1655 when he became a vampire. He met Kristof and Lucinda while they were in Paris, as did I. Lastly, there's Camille. She was twenty-two in 1917 when she became a vampire. Cristó found her hiding in the Paris sewers. Unlike Lucy, she'd been taught not just the basics, but how to survive unnoticed and had lived with her creator for many years until the woman grew tired of her companionship and left, taking everything and leaving Camille nowhere to live. Without somewhere to go,

78

she'd taken to hiding in the sewers until she met Cristó. They fell in love and shortly after, they met Kristof and Lucinda and the foursome have travelled together for many of the years since."

"You said you met them in Paris, too. Was it at the same time?"

"Sort of. I met them but didn't stay with them. I was angry at being who I was for a lot of years and I would seek out wars and join them, fighting for whatever side I felt was more right. I was in France fighting in the Second World War, on the side of the English when I ran into Kristof and Lucinda. I knew straight away they were vampires. We can always tell our own kind. Then, just before the war ended, I disappeared, knowing that in war I would simply be listed as MIA and no-one would look too hard for me, particularly as I had no living family who knew of me. Many years later, elsewhere in Europe, I ran into them again. They'd met Cristóbal and Camille in the intervening years and were all travelling together. That's when I joined them for a while."

"That was a long time ago. Have you been together ever since?"

"No. I went off by myself a few years after that. I believe Cristó and Cami have gone off on their own for a while and then reunited with them also. We all met up again here about three years ago. Kris and Lucy were here first. The big house belongs to Kris. I ran into Cristó and Cami in Spain and we all decided to come here and see Kris and Lucy. Once we were here, Cristó and I enrolled in the university and pretended we met there and became housemates who've become friends. Lucy was already at the uni, so to our uni friends, she's our sort-of-landlord and housemate-come-friend."

"Wow. That's complicated. So, do they know about me?"

"Yes. I told them yesterday."

"What do they think of your human girlfriend?"

"They're cautious. It's never been safe for humans to know we exist. They're afraid you might hurt us all."

"No way. I love you, Dante. I don't want anything bad to ever happen to you."

"I love you too, my beautiful bewitching human girl." He pulled her close and kissed her. Her body tingled and she held him tightly. Her mind was racing. She hadn't meant to say she loved him, it'd just slipped out, but then he said it to her. Lari was overjoyed. She couldn't believe how fast things happened with Dante but they felt right and not rushed.

They talked and kissed until it was almost seven-thirty. "Okay, my Larissa. I promised your father you'd be home safe before nine o'clock and I don't want to screw up on my first proper date with you, so it's time for us to head back to your place now unless I'm allowed to drive at light speed."

Lari sighed. "No to light speed, okay. I wish I could spend all night with you."

"No, you don't. You need sleep and I don't."

"Don't you sleep?"

"No."

"I thought vampires slept in coffins or freezers or something like that."

"Yeah, that's like the garlic and the crosses. Myth. Why do I need sleep? I'm not alive, I'm undead. You sleep because you're alive. Your body regenerates while you sleep. Once every few years or so we kind of... rest... for about twenty-four hours, but it's still not sleep."

He picked her up and carried her back up to the car. She slid off and kissed him again. Suddenly she was struck by shooting pains in her head. Squeezing her eyes shut and clutching her skull, she cried out, "Ouch!"

"Lari? Lari? What's wrong?" There was panic edging his voice.

"Ohhh," she groaned. "Headache. I get killer headaches sometimes. Hang on and hopefully it'll go soon." She stood still, clutching her head with her eyes squeezed shut. He could see her lips moving but she wasn't speaking.

Finally a few minutes later she opened her eyes and let her hands drop from her head. "That sucked," she told him. "They've been worse since we moved here. I think it's the change in climate."

"Are you sure you're okay now?" he asked looking concerned.

"Yeah, it's okay. There's just a dull throb in the back of my skull. I'll be okay." She reached up and put her arms around his neck, planting a kiss on him. "Thank you for caring."

TWENTY-ONE

He got her home with nearly half an hour to spare and her parents were thrilled. She gave him her home and mobile numbers before she got out of the car and because her parents knew she was out with him, didn't bother taking his jacket off. He promised to call her after school finished tomorrow and she kissed him goodnight in the car.

Of course, her parents wanted to know all about her sightseeing day, where she'd been, what they'd eaten. She told them about the Barossa Valley and how beautiful it looked and how he'd packed a picnic basket for them full of seafood and salads and cans of soft drink.

She told them how they went for another drive down to Cape Jervois but made it sound like they walked around doing the tourist thing and never mentioned their hiding place in the rocks.

Lari's mother looked at her father, who nodded. "Lari, he really seems like a nice boy and your father and I've had a talk about this. Clearly you like him a lot and he feels the same way about you. Whose idea was it for him to meet us?"

"Both of us, I guess."

"Okay. That's honest. We won't pretend it doesn't worry us that he's nineteen and I know you think it's only three years and in a lot of ways you can be mature for your age, but those are still three big years. A lot changes between sixteen and nineteen. A lot of growing up happens." She smiled at Lari to soften her words, and then continued, "But boys do take longer to mature than girls so we'll consider that subject done for now. Okay?" She looked at Lari, who smiled and nodded. "Good. Next thing. He has a very fast sports car but he told us he doesn't drink. Is that true?"

"Mum, Dad, he does not touch alcohol. He said he thinks it tastes terrible."

"I hope you're telling us the truth there. Your father and I know there are plenty of teens that do and we're glad you're interested in one who doesn't. Whatever happens, I want you to promise us that you won't ever get into his car with him if he's been drinking. Promise?"

"Easy promise, mum. He really doesn't drink alcohol. I promise to never ever get into his car with him if he's been drinking alcohol."

"Good." Her mother smiled. "Okay, last few things. You've obviously spent some time with him down the beach so he shares your interest in surfing. He seems intelligent and he was very polite. Your father and I liked him. All right, here goes." Lari's mother took a deep breath and continued, "We think we've brought you up well, so we're going to show you some trust here. There are rules, though."

"What are the rules?"

"Okay. We don't want you two rushing things. You and Dante can see each other on Friday and Saturday nights as long as you're home before eleven o'clock. On weeknights and Sunday nights we want you home before seven-thirty and that goes for when you're with Dante or other friends. Come home straight after school unless we've agreed to something else. Homework done before you go anywhere. If your grades start slipping, we start curtailing your social life. Always take your phone when you're not home and make sure it's charged. Is that all right with you?"

"Oh yes, Mum! Thanks Mum! Thanks Dad! You won't regret this."

"I hope not!"

Larissa threw her arms around each of her parents, hugging them both. "I'm going to bed now since I have to start school tomorrow. Goodnight and really, thanks! I'm so happy now."

"Goodnight, honey," her Dad told her. "I'm glad you're starting to like living here."

"Goodnight, Lari," her Mum echoed. "What time do you want me to wake you?"

"School starts at eight-thirty?" Her mother nodded. "Then wake me at seven, thanks Mum."

"All right. Sweet dreams."

"Night." Lari waved and went to her room feeling light as a feather. She couldn't stop grinning. Dante had told her he loved her and her parents said she could see him. It was almost enough to make her forget her fear of starting at her new school.

She flicked on her iPod and turned the volume down low so her parents wouldn't come in to tell her off. She didn't want to aggravate them when they were being so cool about Dante.

Changing into her blue pyjamas, she sprawled on her bed and went over the day's events in her head. She enjoyed snuggling next to him in the Barossa Valley while they kissed and he answered her questions. For a moment, just before he pulled away from her, all she'd been able to think was how much she wanted him to make love to her and that excited and scared her all at once. And it was so cute how he'd put together the picnic basket for her. She would have to tell Ebony about that tomorrow when she rang.

Larissa gasped as she remembered Ebony was supposed to call her today only she'd been out with Dante. She looked at her clock. It was only just past nine o'clock but they were half an hour behind Sydney. She raced out to the family room where her parents were still watching TV.

"Mum! Can I ring Ebony? She was supposed to call me today. I promise I won't be on the phone long!"

"Lari, it's gone nine o'clock..." her mother looked doubtfully at her father, who stared resolutely at the television screen. "Oh, damn! I nearly forgot to tell you. She rang about six and I told her you were out." She looked at Lari's pleading eyes. "Oh, all right. Just this once. But keep it short."

"Thanks, Mum!" Larissa grabbed the cordless and bolted back to her room, dialling Ebony on the way.

It was answered on the third ring. "Hi?"

"Ebony, were you sitting on that thing?" laughed Larissa. "Sorry it's so late but guess what?" She flung herself back onto the bed.

"What?"

"I had a proper date with Dante. He met Mum and Dad today and they said we could go out till nine o'clock so he took me to the Barossa and made a picnic basket for me and then we went to Cape Jervois and I had the best time!"

"Oh, I'm so rapt for you! I had a great night last night with Mark and Sera and Pete. We're doing it again next weekend. We went to the movies but I wasn't really watching much coz Mark was kissing me and I liked it."

"Cool. So are you and Mark an item now?"

"Yeah. He asked me if I wanted to be his girlfriend and I said yes. He drove us all home in his car. It's a Ford. I don't know what kind." She giggled. "You know me, I'm crap with cars. It has four doors and it was red."

"Oh, Ebony! I have to tell you about Dante's car! The colour's so cool! It's black and it has like flaky metallic bits in it and it's a 370Z. Dad was impressed. I like it and it goes really fast. He told Dad it's six months old."

"Dante has a new 370Z? Even I know what they are... Oh, they just look so wicked! Is he rich or something?"

"Yeah, I think he's got lots of money."

"Oh, wow. He's cute and rich. You are so lucky."

There was a knock on her door and her mother's face peered in. "Lari, time to say goodbye. You can talk to each other tomorrow after school."

Larissa put her hand over the phone's mouthpiece. "Okay Mum. Five minutes. I promise."

"Five minutes," her mother answered, leaving and shutting the door behind her.

"Ebony, I gotta go. Mum just came in and told me to hang up. Ring me tomorrow after seven-thirty, okay? I'm allowed out till then and Dante's ringing me after school."

"Okay, seven-thirty my time or seven-thirty yours?"

"Seven-thirty mine, so eight yours. Bye Ebony. We've both got boyfriends!" Both girls squealed with delight.

"Bye Lari. Talk to you tomorrow."

They hung up and Lari took the phone back to the family room, saying thanks and goodnight again to her parents before heading back to her room.

Sprawled on her bed again, Larissa giggled quietly as she remembered his face in the car when she asked him about sex and how after she'd said she wanted to know if it could be done and if he would do it with her, he'd told her he was afraid of hurting her if they had sex. But he also said it was possible. On the hill while he was kissing her, she didn't want him to stop. She thought about it and decided she wanted her first time to be with Dante. He made her tingle all over. Part of her was desperate to lose her virginity to him, even though he'd told her it might hurt. Lari reassured herself that it would hurt anyway since she was a virgin.

She'd enjoyed the Barossa Valley but the cave at the Cape was still her favourite place since it was the first place he'd ever taken her and it felt secret and special, and it was there he told her how he became a vampire. Imagine him knowing her great-great-great grandpa and being his friend and now he was her boyfriend. It was mad. She remembered his stories about his vampire housemate friends. Larissa wondered if she'd ever meet them, if she'd already met them and just didn't know they were vampires, like she didn't know about Dante till he told her.

She thought it was cool that they could tell if someone else was a vampire and she decided that next time they were together she'd ask him how they knew.

Her eyes were getting tired and she had school tomorrow so she crawled under her quilt and closed her eyes, remembering Dante's kisses as she was drifting off to sleep.

TWENTY-TWO

She woke to her mother telling her it was after seven. "I'm awake," she told her mother as she opened her eyes. Her mother walked out and Larissa sighed. She still felt sleepy and when she sat up her head hammered. "Bloody stupid headaches," she muttered as she dragged herself out of bed.

She pulled a bath sheet out of the linen press and turned the shower on so that the jets hammered out, making the bathroom hot and steamy. A few minutes under the steaming water and her head felt better.

Finished with her shower, she headed back into her room to dress in one of the white t-shirts with the school logo that her mother had bought and a pair of skinny denim jeans. Looking out the window at grey skies, she grabbed the blue school windcheater from her closet and pulled it on over the top. Larissa dug her favourite sneakers out from the bottom of her closet and put them on.

Having already seen how well-groomed Melanie and Lisa were, she blow-dried her hair and raked her unruly curls into something tamer and since Dante had told her he liked it loose and the school dress code didn't enforce her braiding her hair, she left it flowing. She could even wear make-up to school, so she quickly made up her face and finally went out to the kitchen for breakfast.

Her stomach was churning with nerves and she hoped her mother wasn't expecting her to eat a hearty breakfast.

"Cereal or toast, Lari? You took so long getting ready you're almost out of time."

"Toast. And juice, please."

Her mother popped two slices of bread in the toaster and poured her a glass of orange juice. Lari sat at the bench and hoped for her stomach to settle and the headache to stay gone.

She sipped her juice and when the toast popped, buttered it thickly and spread it with crunchy peanut butter. She felt sick eating but she forced the two slices down just in time for her mother to round up her and Brad and hustle them into the car.

She was carrying her backpack although it was empty except for a pencil case filled with an assortment of pens, pencils, erasers and sharpeners and a ring binder holding a wad of blank lined paper. She'd collect her books from the school once she was there.

Her mother drove them to the Eastern campus. She parked in the visitor's space in the car park and left Brad waiting in the car and listening to the radio while she enrolled Larissa.

The process didn't take too long as her mother had started it all before they left Sydney and most of her paperwork was already there. Larissa collected her booklist and her mother paid the outstanding amount so Lari could just go collect the books.

She got a timetable for her classes and a map showing her where to go. The bell rang for first period while she was still filling out forms and waiting for permission to go.

"I'll take you to the book room and then once that's sorted, I'll give you a short tour and take you to second period. You have most of your classes on the western campus. We allow five minutes to get between lessons. The first bell signals the end of class and the second bell signals the beginning of the next class. The only times there's one bell is first period and last period." The teacher's aide explained as she highlighted different things on her timetable.

"Toilets?" asked Larissa.

The aide pointed at several locations on the map. "You need a pass if you're going to the toilets during class time. The mall across the road is out of bounds unless you have a pass allowing you to be there at lunchtime."

The teacher's aide looked at Larissa. "Do you need the toilets now? We can make that our first stop."

"Ah, no, I'm okay."

"Fine."

Deb appeared from the office. "Okay, everything's done. You'll be all right. I have to go enrol Brad now. Love you, baby. Have a good first day." Her mother kissed her and left through the front entrance. Lari wanted to bolt after her but she knew it wouldn't be smart.

"This way, Larissa."

"Lari," Larissa told her. "I don't get called Larissa, I get called Lari."

"Okay, Lari, it is." The teacher's aide made a note on her file. "Follow me, please," she requested, striding down the hall.

The rest of first period was spent getting her books together and doing a fast tour of the east and west campuses. She knew she wouldn't remember everything and expected to get lost a lot in her first week. The good news was that there was a canteen on each campus and the school had huge ovals so there was probably a lot of sport.

Larissa hoped that hockey was one of the sports as she'd been team captain for hockey at her last school. Surfing, hockey, ice-skating and roller-skating were her favourite sports and since surfing and skating weren't usually school sports, she hoped this school offered hockey like her last.

The bell for end of first period sounded and her guide led her to her second period class. Larissa glanced at her timetable. It was Math. She hated Math but she was good at it. Before the second bell rang, she was standing at the desk of her new Math teacher, Mr Henley, and being introduced.

"I don't do assigned seating, Larissa."

"Lari," she interrupted. "It should say Lari coz that's what everyone calls me."

He pulled a slight face and made a note in his papers. "Lari, then. I let my students choose their seats and you can choose differently every time you have my class if that's your desire. So, please sit anywhere."

"Ta, Mr Henley." Lari looked around and picked a table at the back of the room. It would be harder to get stared at if she was sitting at the back. Of course, she didn't count on the fact that she was one of the early arrivals to class and every student entering the room paused to take a good look at her. She half-smiled at each of them.

Second bell sounded and most of the seats were filled. "Quiet! Quiet!" called Mr Henley. "Right, you've all noticed we have a new student. Her name is Lari and she's come to us from Sydney. Please welcome her."

There was a round of soft applause and a sea of faces turned to stare at her.

"Yes, yes, that'll do," Mr Henley announced, "Math is the subject now so let's focus." He began writing on the board while he spoke and Lari quickly pulled out her Math textbook and started scribbling notes.

The rest of the day was a blur of bells and classes and she was relieved when it was over. Melanie and Lisa found her in English class just before lunch and led her around, ending her getting lost for the day. It was a relief to have them fielding the endless curiosity about her and at lunch she sat with them and their circle of friends.

Finally the last bell rang and she walked home. Melanie and Lisa accompanied her most of the way, turning off a block from her place. She promised to meet up with them the next day at school and finally started to relax when her house was in sight.

The phone rang ten minutes after she walked in the door and her mother called out, "Lari! Dante's on the phone for you."

She grabbed the phone from her mother. "Thanks. I'll take it in my room." She turned and walked to her room, "Dante! You rang!"

87

TWENTY-THREE

"How was your first day at school?" he asked.

"Uggh. I got stared at and lost and it pretty much sucked. And the worst thing is I have to go back again tomorrow."

"Funny."

"Yeah, I'm a hoot. You sound different."

"Different? From what?"

"The way you talk on the phone is different." She paused and thought for a bit. "You're not so talkative."

"Oh. I'm just not used to chatting on a phone. Never had to do it before. You're my first human girlfriend since the invention of phones."

"Ha! Who's funny now?" she laughed. "Okay, my 'rents said I can see you after school any day as long as I go home and get my homework done first. So, I'm home and I have no homework to do today coz I finished the little bit they assigned during break times. Wanna meet me somewhere? Please... I want hugs and kisses from you. Oh yeah, I have to be back home by seven-thirty."

"How about I pick you up? I can see the water from here and there's no surf and the beach looks ugly."

"Cool. I'm ready when you are."

"Okay, see you in five minutes."

"'Kay," she smiled as she hung up, taking the phone back to the family room. "Hey Mum, I've got no homework tonight and Dante's coming to pick me up. I'll be home before seven-thirty."

"Okay," her mother replied. "Where are you two going?"

"Ummn, somewhere for food."

"That's vague."

"He didn't say exactly." She waved her mobile. "I'll have my phone with me like you asked."

"All right. Don't go too far and have a good time," her mother told her as Dante's car pulled up out front. Deb watched through the window as he got out and walked to the door while Larissa raced to the entrance to meet him.

"Hey!" she greeted him, opening the door before he could knock or ring the bell.

"Hey," he smiled at her. "You don't want me to say hello to your parents?" he asked as she stepped outside.

"Nope. Ya don't have to. Dad's not home yet anyway."

"Okay."

88

She grabbed his hand and leaned against him as he walked her back to his car, opening the door for her. She got in and he walked round to the driver's door, getting behind the wheel and driving off.

"So, beautiful witch, where are we going?"

"Dunno. I thought I'd leave it up to you. But can we get some food later on coz I'm starving. I couldn't hardly eat this morning coz I was so nervous."

"Well, I'll get food for you now if you want. What would you like?"

"Ummnn... how about pizza? I haven't had pizza for ages."

"Sure. That's no problem." He turned towards the hills.

"Aren't we going to the Cape this afternoon?" she asked.

"No. You said you'd leave it up to me so I thought we could go somewhere you haven't been. It's not far and there's pizza nearby."

"Cool. Any hints where?"

"Nope. You can be surprised."

"Okay," she smiled. "Oh, Dante, I just remembered. I thought of some new questions for you. Can I ask them?"

"Sure." He glanced across and smiled when he saw the smile on her face. "What kind of questions are these?"

"Good ones. First question is how do you recognize other vampires coz I wouldn't have known you were a vampire if you hadn't told me."

"That's easy. We can smell each other."

"Really? You can smell? Even though you told me you don't breathe."

"I said we don't have to breathe. We can look like we're breathing, inhaling and exhaling, and we can sniff and smell things. Plus we have a kind of radar in our minds that lets us know when we're near other vampires."

"Wow. Okay, question number two is how often do you need to eat or drink or feed or whatever it is you call it? Actually, question two and a half is what do you call it?"

He laughed. "It can be called feeding or drinking, I guess. I don't think I've heard another vampire call it eating and we don't usually say suck your blood, either," he laughed again. "How often can vary. Sometimes once or twice a week, other times it's daily. Really it depends on how much I've drunk or fed from someone." He looked over at her. "Doesn't this conversation freak you out?"

"Nope." She looked at him and smiled. "You don't have to answer this one if you don't want to. I won't make you. When did you last drink or feed? And what happens if you're thirsty?"

"Okay. I last drank a few nights ago. Night before we first went out. Drank from a few people, more than usual. I was nervous about being with you. I'm not thirsty yet although I probably will want to feed again sometime tomorrow. As for what happens when I'm thirsty... I can smell the blood flowing in people really strongly and y'know what it feels like when you're really thirsty?" He asked her.

"Yes," she answered. "I get a dry mouth and just want a drink."

"Well, that's how I feel only without the dry mouth. I don't think there's any way for you to tell that I'm thirsty but I don't really know. I've never looked at myself when I'm thirsty and I don't let myself get too thirsty."

"You said that you thought sucking... drinking animal blood was gross..."

"Yes?"

"Well, ummnnn... why is it gross? And can't you suck, drink, animal blood instead of human? Like Brad Pitt did in that movie?"

He laughed. "Brad Pitt was pretending to be a vampire. He's not a vampire. And I'm pretty sure he didn't drink any kind of blood for real." Finally he stopped grinning. "Okay. Animal blood won't satisfy the thirst. It has to be human blood. And it doesn't taste the same. It doesn't appeal. That's what I meant by gross."

"One more thing... I am really curious and I'm not sure how to ask you this," She paused, pursing her lips and frowning briefly. "I've thought about what you asked me... about if I wanted you to suck my blood... and I think I do. I don't want you to do it heaps but I want you to do it once so I know what it feels like."

"Yeah, that's not going to happen," he told her. "I said I don't think of you as food and I won't drink from you."

"Please, can you do it when you're not thirsty so you're just doing it for the pleasure thing? You said there's pleasure in it."

"Larissa. Please. You don't know what you're asking."

"What do you mean?"

"There's this thing, like an imaginary line, and I don't want to cross it. You're the only human girlfriend I've had since I became a vampire and not drinking from you is one of the things that makes you special and different from all the rest of humanity. Please don't ask me to do this. And I... it's hard enough, don't make it harder. I'm afraid of drinking from you and... Please, Lari. Don't ask this."

"Okay. For now." The sun was slowly sinking to the west making the sky a vivid orange. "So, where are we now?" she asked, changing the subject.

"Near Goolwa. There's a beach and some dunes. You'll see. About five kilometres further and we'll be there."

"Oh."

90

"Lari, don't sound so disappointed in me."

"I'm not. Really, I'm not. It's just been such a long day."

He looked disbelieving but said nothing more and they drove the last five kilometres listening to the latest Arctic Monkeys CD pouring through the speakers.

TWENTY-FOUR

"We're here," he told her, parking the car in a large carpark at the foreshore. She got out of the car and looked around her. The sun still had a way to go before it set and the water looked like it was on fire, reflecting the orange light. "Hey, that looks pretty wicked."

"Thought you'd like it." He took her hand and led her away. "Walk this way, beautiful." He led her to the rolling dunes next to the carpark that were partially covered in native vegetation. A few minutes later they'd slipped over the crest and disappeared into a hollow.

"Oh, this is way cool!"

"You like it?" he asked.

"Yeah, it's fully sick."

"Great." He sat down and pulled her to the sand. "You said you wanted hugs and kisses. They're available now if you still want them."

"Of course I do," she told him, snuggling against him. "I think I'm getting used to your chilliness. It doesn't feel as cold anymore."

He chuckled and pulled her onto him as he lay down on his back. Instantly she kissed him, gently at first and then more passionately. She slid her hands from his face to his chest, then to his hips, slipping them up inside his t-shirt. His skin felt cool and smooth and like a muscular moving statue.

"Ohh," he groaned softly but he kept kissing her. His own hands found their way to her breasts, staying outside her t-shirt. He stopped moving.

She heard herself moaning with pleasure and pressed herself harder against him. Without warning he propelled her off him and leapt away. She landed hard on the ground and was stunned to see he was nearly six feet from her.

"No!" he told her. He stared at her, his eyes wild. "I'm sorry. I didn't mean to scare you, hurt you. We have to stop."

She was panting heavily. "I wasn't scared and I'm not hurt. I liked it."

"I meant when I pushed you away."

"Oh," she answered. "I still wasn't scared. Didn't want to stop, but I wasn't scared. Or hurt."

"Lari. I told you. I'm not sure about this. You're so fragile. I don't want to hurt you or break you. Please. You're making it so hard for me today. Asking me to drink from you. Trying to make me get more physical than I'm ready for."

"I'm sorry. I'll behave. I promise. Just cuddle me again, please."

He moved closer to her, taking her hand and kneeling next to her. "I love you, Larissa. I really don't want to do anything to hurt you."

"I know. I love you too, Dante." He kissed her again, gently, and her heart sang with pleasure. "I feel like we've known each other forever. I can't believe we only met a week ago."

"Come on, baby, let's get that pizza for you," he changed the subject and lifted her with him as he stood. Together they walked back to the car and drove back into town to the pizza bar, ordering her a small vegetarian, garlic bread, and a can of drink. Then they returned to the beach so she could eat in the dunes and no-one would notice that he ate nothing. "Did you order the garlic bread so you could test it out on me?" he asked her.

"Nope. You said it has no effect and I like it so I figured if it has no effect on you, then I can eat it."

He kissed her immediately she ate a mouthful of garlic bread, as if to prove the point.

"Strong," he told her, raising an eyebrow. "There must be a whole garlic clove in that!"

"Aha, you're still here and look like you. Nothing strange is happening. Damn, it must be a myth then!" she laughed, biting into a slice of pizza.

He moved behind her and nuzzled the back of her neck. His hands slipped around her waist. He slowly moved his hands upwards, still kissing the back of her neck. Larissa stayed really still and kept eating her slice of pizza, afraid he'd stop again. His hands continued their journey to her breasts and she gasped softly with pleasure. She stopped eating and closed her eyes, her breath getting ragged as he gently brushed across her nipples.

She felt an ache inside, a longing to feel him inside her. "Dante," she whispered, surprised at how husky her voice sounded. She didn't realize she'd dropped her slice of pizza or that her fingers were digging furrows in the sand.

"Larissa, my Larissa," he whispered into the back of her neck.

"I love you, Dante, with all my heart," she whispered, leaning back into him.

"Stay still, please, my love. I don't want to do anything to hurt you, but I want to try something..."

He slid one of his hands down her body, reaching between her thighs and pausing there. She moaned. Her back arched and she pressed against him. His other hand kept teasing her nipple through the fabric. She'd never felt this level of pleasure before.

She felt his sharp teeth bite her where her neck and shoulder met, a quick nip, and waves of hot pleasure flowed over her. "Oh Dante!" she gasped.

"Larissa!" he whispered in a husky voice. "You are so beautiful, my Larissa!" His teeth were no longer against her skin, his hands had stopped moving and he was very still against her. "This is enough for now. I don't trust myself to do more," he whispered into her ear, his voice still throaty.

"Oh Dante, yes, it's enough. I love you so much." She leaned into him, her body limp and relaxed.

They stayed like that for a while until Dante told her it was time to leave in order to keep her curfew. Reluctantly she stood up and walked with him to the car. She snuggled against him all the way home and passionately kissed him goodbye, extracting a promise from him that he'd pick her up again tomorrow after school.

TWENTY-FIVE

The next six weeks passed in a blur of school and passionate encounters with Dante. They mostly alternated between the cave at Cape Jervois and the dunes by the beach in Goolwa. He took her ice-skating for their first Saturday night date. They spent days and nights surfing when the waves were good. Each time they went to the Cape they sat and talked, kissing and cuddling in between. Every visit to the dunes resulted in them experimenting with how far they could go physically.

He'd bitten her three or four times since that first time and each time he nipped her, he froze and called a halt to everything. He told her it was because he only bit her when he forgot himself and he was afraid to do that with her.

He still hadn't drunk her blood. He adamantly refused to and she'd agreed to stop asking. Pushing the boundaries with the physical stuff was her reward for not asking him to drink from her.

She'd tried to find out if there was anything about him in the family records but it was hard when she couldn't tell anyone why. Her mother was curious about her sudden interest in the family history and Lari told her it was sparked because Dante's family was from Whitby and so was her mother's side of the family. So far she hadn't discovered anything about him, although he'd been pleased to hear about James and Fanny and the three children they'd had.

In no time it was October and her sixteenth birthday on the eighth. Her parents had planned a party for her and Dante was part of it. He wouldn't tell her the plan no matter how much she asked, pleaded or cajoled.

Her headaches hadn't eased off. If anything, they were getting more frequent, especially in the mornings. Dante worried about them but she told him that she'd had headaches for years and was used to them.

This year her birthday fell on a Saturday and she woke with her head hammering. She groaned and dragged herself to the bathroom. Larissa felt better after her shower but she was so nervous about what they had planned for her that she couldn't eat.

Dante arrived about nine to take her somewhere. She knew it was to get her out of the house while her parents readied it for the party they'd arranged, but she was sure Dante had something planned for her as well.

He drove her to the Barossa Valley. They hadn't been there since their first picnic. They walked up the same hill and sat down at its crest. He leaned over and kissed her. "Happy Sweet Sixteen, my Larissa," he whispered as his lips hovered over hers.

She smiled. "What do I get for my birthday then?" she asked cheekily.

He reached into his pocket and pulled out a small gift-wrapped box.

She took it eagerly, tearing the wrapping off to reveal a velvet jewel box. Opening it she found a silver filigree locket that held a photo of her and a photo of him. "Oh, Dante! It's just perfect!" She flung her arms around him and kissed him deeply. "Put it on me, please!" she demanded.

He obligingly fastened the locket around her neck. She smiled as she stared into his eyes and he smiled back at her. "I love you," he told her.

"I love you, too," she answered.

He moved so fast she didn't see anything, just felt his lips against hers. Then she was falling backwards. He twisted as they went down, somehow ending up under her.

His hands seemed to be everywhere and she felt waves of pleasure overtake her.

"Dante..." she moaned. He pushed her away from him. "I'm sixteen now, Dante," she told him in a husky voice. "Please, can we? You know..." She smiled at him. "I want you to do it."

"Lari... I'm afraid of hurting you." He was still holding her at arm's length, his eyes looking seriously into hers.

"Please, Dante..." she pleaded. She leaned into him and kissed him. The kiss grew deeper and more passionate and he relaxed his hold on her, letting her fall onto him.

His hands slid from her waist to her hips and then returned to her waist to undo her jeans, pulling them off her. It was the furthest they'd ever gone. He'd always insisted she keep her clothes on before. She didn't know how he did it but somehow her top was gone as well, and now she was wearing only her underwear.

Lari arched her back, pressing her hips into him, and he kissed the part of her breast visible above the bra. She clasped his head, holding him tight against her as she felt a burning desire to have him inside her. "Dante, please... I love you..." she whispered.

He pulled his head away and stared into her eyes as he removed her bra and panties and she realized that he'd removed his clothes also. There was a searing, burning pain that was equalled by the pleasure she felt as she realized he was finally making love to her.

A kaleidoscope of fireworks exploded in her mind at the exact moment he sunk his sharp teeth into her breast.

A while later she woke to find that he was no longer inside her but she was still wrapped in his arms. Lari was acutely aware of her vajayjay that felt like it was on fire and almost wished for some ice to take away the burning sensation, but more than that, she was overwhelmingly blissfully happy. "Oh Dante, that was the best birthday present ever!"

He looked serious. "I bit you. I'm sorry."

"Did you drink?"

"A little. I stopped myself."

"Is that why I flaked?"

"No. Your eyes rolled back in your head and you passed out." He paused as if considering what he was going to say next. "I was worried. If you hadn't come to then I was going to rush you to a hospital."

"Well, that would've been silly. What would you say? I'm a vampire and we just made love for the first time and now she's flaked?"

He raised his eyebrows at her. "When you put it that way..." He kept a tight hold of her, "Beautiful Larissa... I want you to get a doctor to check out your headaches. They worry me. Today, the... flaking out... it worries me. Please. Do it for me."

She rolled her eyes. "Okay. But not today. Today is my birthday and no doctor is a part of it." It occurred to her then that he'd told her he'd drunk her blood. "You drank and I don't remember it. That's not fair or is that how it always works?"

"Way to change the subject. I drank a little and you should remember it because I told you I wouldn't ever use mind control on you. And I didn't mean to do it. I lost control."

"You got control back coz you said you stopped."

"Yes, I did." He paused. "Did I hurt you too badly?"

"No." He looked doubtful so she continued, "Well, okay, maybe it hurt a bit coz it was my first time and all, but that was beautiful and so much better than I ever imagined and you've made me so happy."

"Are you lying to me?"

"What? You don't think I was a virgin?"

He laughed. "Cheeky witch! That's not what I meant and you know it."

"I remember you biting my breast but that's all. Why don't I remember, Dante?"

"I don't know. Maybe it has something to do with you passing out the way you did. They happened about the same time. You screamed my name and then your eyes rolled back in your head and your body went rigid and then limp."

"Oh." Larissa didn't know what to tell him. "So, changing the subject again. What's the deal with this party?"

He shook his head. "I promised your parents that I wouldn't tell and I won't. But I should be getting you back now. I only had to keep you away until mid afternoon."

"What time is it?" she asked.

"Just after midday."

"How do you always know the time without a watch or looking at a clock?"

"I don't know it exactly. I'm just close."

"Still... how do you know?"

"I don't know. Maybe it's because I came from a time where we still worked out the hour with sundials and by looking at the sky. And before you ask, yes there were clocks and watches but they were expensive. Sundials were still relatively common and not everybody wore a watch."

He finally let go of her and sat up, pulling his clothes on. Larissa sneaked a look at him before he got fully dressed. His skin was like marble and he looked like a living statue, almost too perfect. He took her breath away without even doing anything.

He tossed her clothes to her and she started getting dressed. It took her much longer to put her clothes on than it had for him to remove them. He stood and held out his hand to help her. She grabbed his hand, grateful for the assistance when she realized she felt dizzy as she stood. He caught her before she could fall, that same worried look on his face again. "Lari, you almost looked like you were going to pass out again."

"Just dizzy. It's nothing. Don't make it a big deal."

TWENTY-SIX

There were cars lining her street when she got home. Apparently her dad had told Dante to park in the drive because he opened the gate and pulled in for the first time since they'd been seeing each other.

Lari was getting out of the car as her mother rushed out to greet her. "Happy Sixteenth, Lari!" she called as she threw her arms around her. "Come inside, your friends are already here!" She turned to Dante, "Thanks for taking her out this morning so we could get things done."

"No problems, Mrs Parker," he smiled.

Lari showed her mother the locket. "Look what Dante gave me, Mum!"

"Oh, that's beautiful. Come say hello to your friends." Deb grabbed Lari's hand and led her into the house and out the back where her friends were waiting.

"Happy Birthday!" they chorused as she walked out the back door. "Hip, hip, hooray!"

"Thank you, thank you!" Lari was smiling and blushing, looking around for Dante and spying him standing just behind her with a smile on his face.

Her parents had decorated the yard with streamers and balloons and a giant sign proclaiming "Happy Birthday" in foil letters.

Her dad was standing over the barbecue, cooking, and there was a long trestle table loaded with salads and snacks. "Drinks are in the laundry, sweetie," her dad called to her, waving his tongs. "Happy Birthday!" Brad was standing next to him, helping.

Melanie and Lisa rushed over to her, demanding to give her their presents first. Quickly she unwrapped the gifts. Melanie had bought her a new hoodie in dark blue and Lisa had bought her a new baseball cap and some cool-smelling surf wax for her board.

"Oh, thanks guys! These are fantastic!" She hugged her two new best friends and got to work opening the other gifts as they were presented to her. Dante had got her a can of cola and handed it to her and was quietly sitting beside her on the deck as she unwrapped presents and thanked her friends. Eventually she reached the end of the gifts and could relax. She leaned against Dante, "Can I leave now?" she whispered to him.

He laughed softly, "Nope. Your parents are yet to give you anything. Guess that means you're stuck here a while longer."

"Grrrr," she growled, kissing his neck.

Her mother chose that moment to walk over to her. "Lari, ready to see what your father, brother, and I got you?"

"Yeah, Mum, that'd be cool."

"Brad!" her mother called, waving him over. Brad came running. "It's time. Go get Lari's present, please."

Her brother smiled and ran into the house, returning a few minutes later with a windsurfing board with a big ribbon tied around it.

"A sailboard?" Lari asked. She smiled. "Oh, wow! That's awesome! Thanks!"

"It's got a mast and sails, too, Lari. They're still inside. I just couldn't carry it all at once," her brother explained.

"Thanks!" she hugged her mother and then her brother.

"Yuk. You can stop that, sis," he said. "Here, take it."

She took the board from him and he bolted back to the barbecue to help her dad. "I have to say thanks to Dad, too," she told her mum.

"Here, I'll take it," Dante told her, taking the board from her and leaning it up against the wall.

"Thanks," she smiled at him and then ran to hug her father. He beamed at her and went back to his cooking.

The party continued for the rest of the afternoon. The birthday cake came out at six-thirty, her favourite black forest torte loaded with candles and everyone sang Happy Birthday to her. The party ended just after seven with everyone telling her it was a great day as they left. Larissa felt incredibly tired but decided that was due to her activities with Dante before the party started and then the excitement of the afternoon.

Dante was giving her that worried look again as she wobbled across the deck, scooping up some of the rubbish. "What?" she asked him with a frown.

"You seem a bit unsteady," he told her.

"Tired. Big day," she told him.

"Do you want me to go so you can have an early night, then?" he asked.

"No way. It's my birthday still and a Saturday night. We've got till eleven o'clock."

"Larissa, leave that, honey. Your dad and I will clean up. Go out with Dante and enjoy yourself. Midnight curfew tonight since it's your birthday." Her mother walked out onto the deck, unintentionally interrupting their conversation.

"Okay, Mum. Thanks." Larissa smiled at her mother and turned to Dante, sticking out her tongue. "Let's go, Dante."

He smiled and followed her out to his car. They got in and he asked her, "So, where to?"

"Dunno. The dunes?"

100

He raised an eyebrow at her. "Didn't you have enough of that this morning?"

"Nope. Never." She smiled at him. "It's my birthday and I want more."

"Ha," he told her, starting the engine. "Not going to happen tonight." He drove out and headed south.

"Are we going to Cape Jervois?"

"Yes."

"Oh," she paused. "You're mean."

He snorted. "I am not. Mean is what you can be, my beautiful little witch. You know how hard it is for me to control myself and not accidentally hurt you and yet you don't stop pushing me for more." He turned and smiled at her as he finished speaking.

"Watch the road! You know it scares the crap out of me when you don't!" she told him. "And I'm never mean to you. I love you too much."

He snorted again. "God, I love you, Larissa... and you are frequently mean to me." He laughed. "I wish I could ask you to never leave me but I know that's too much. You're only sixteen. You should date some real boys your age, not an old vampire like me."

Larissa's eyes grew wide and she stared at him. "Don't you ever say anything like that! It makes me think you're gonna break up with me, leave me. Don't you ever leave me. I couldn't stand it. I'd die without you. And you're not an old vampire. You're a young vampire who's been around a lot of years and the most beautiful lover I could ever have."

He looked across at her and smiled. "My beautiful Larissa. I promise I'm not leaving you and I'm not trying to break up with you. Please don't look so... so... like you're going to cry."

"Watch the road!" she squealed. He smiled and turned his eyes back to the road. "I'm not going to cry," she said petulantly, staring out at the road.

"Good." He kept his eyes on the road. "I couldn't stand it if I made you cry. I mean it when I tell you I don't want to hurt you. In any way, Larissa. I really do not want to hurt you ever."

"Then don't talk about us breaking up. Ever. Promise me. I don't like it."

"I promise," he told her quietly.

TWENTY-SEVEN

Larissa woke Sunday morning with another thumping headache. Her clock said it was nearly ten o'clock and for some reason she felt utterly exhausted. Dante was coming to collect her about eleven and they were going somewhere new. He hadn't told her where yet, saying only that they'd get to give her new board a workout. Larissa hoped it was somewhere private where they could get romantic as well. Now that he'd finally crossed that line, she wanted to do it again.

She got up and flashes of light streaked across her eyes in time with the waves of pain that lashed her head. "Stupid headaches. I hate these stupid things. Why do I have to always get them?" she muttered.

She stood up and nearly blacked out, grabbing the edge of her headboard to steady herself. "Uh oh, migraine coming," she whispered. "Go away headache. You're not welcome. I have plans," she instructed her throbbing head in the same low whisper. Certain that her balance had returned, she headed for the shower so she could be ready when Dante arrived, hopefully headache-free.

She showered quickly and dressed in cut-off jeans and a t-shirt. The spring weather had finally arrived and it was forecast to be a beautiful twenty-five degrees.

Her mother was in the kitchen when she finally made her way out there. Her head was still aching, only not quite as violently. "Cereal or toast, Lari?" her mother greeted her.

"Ummmnnn..." she actually felt a bit sick, probably from the headache. "I kind of feel like fruit, actually. Can I have an apple?"

"That's not enough to start the day," her mother admonished.

"I'll work out what I want after the apple, okay?" she compromised.

"All right." Her mother handed her a red-skinned apple and Lari sat at the bench eating it. The clock said it was nearly eleven. Right on cue, Dante's car pulled up out front. "I'll let him in, Lari. You work out what else you're going to eat before you leave here."

Lari was still struggling to finish the apple when Dante followed her mother into the kitchen. She smiled and stood to greet him and her head felt like it was going to split open.

She saw flashes of fire in front of her eyes and a look of horror on the faces of both her mother and Dante and then her world went dark.

She opened her eyes to blank white walls. It felt like there was something on her face. She turned her head and saw her mother and Dante sitting and staring anxiously at her. There was something partially blocking her view.

"Oh, baby, you're awake," her mother got up and stroked her face. "Ssshhh..." she told her as Lari tried to speak. "Don't try to talk, sweetie. The doctors have a mask on you, giving you oxygen."

"Dante?" she whispered into the mask.

"I'm here, Larissa," he told her, getting up and standing next to the bed.

She sighed, her eyes closing involuntarily. She lifted her hand, trying to tell him she wanted to touch him. He seemed to understand and took hold of her hand. "Sorry, I messed up," she whispered, her eyes still closed, not sure if she was actually speaking or just thinking the words. She wanted to open her eyes but they didn't seem to be doing what she wanted.

Finally she got her eyes open and her mother wasn't there. Dante was still holding her hand, only now he was sitting in the chair her mother had vacated. The mask had gone from her face.

"You're awake," he told her, his face looking serious.

"Was I asleep?" she asked.

"Unconscious," he answered.

"Oh." Larissa looked around, taking in her surroundings. "I'm in hospital?" she asked him.

"Yes. Do you remember what happened, Lari?"

"Mum let you in and I said hi and then my head exploded and that's all I remember... oh, except I think I remember you and Mum sitting here."

"Okay. Your mother let me in and you didn't say hi. You stood up and your eyes rolled back in your head, just like the other day, only this time your body started shaking and you crashed to the ground. I should've caught you. I'm so sorry. I froze."

"It's okay. How come I'm here?"

"Your mother called an ambulance. You were unconscious and you kept shaking. I held you while we waited and then the ambulance brought you here. I drove your mother here and stayed. We've been sitting with you for hours. She's talking to the doctors now. They've run a heap of tests on you already and I think they're planning more."

"Oh." Larissa was quiet. She still felt so lethargic. "I feel kinda knackered. Can you hug me, Dante? I'm such a stupid girlfriend. I ruined our day."

"No, you're not," he told her as he gently scooped her into his arms, kissing the top of her head. He lowered her back onto the bed and took her hand again.

"What's wrong with me, Dante?"

He stroked her face, looking sad and serious. "I should let your mother tell you that."

"Please, Dante," she pleaded.

"It's something to do with those headaches you get. Lari, I'm not saying anymore. Your mother's talking to the doctors now. Wait to hear what she has to say."

"Oh," she closed her eyes so she wouldn't cry. Tears seemed to want to happen and she had no idea why.

"Are you okay? Larissa?" Dante sounded worried, almost panicked.

"Yes. I wanna leave."

"No," he sounded firm. "You'll stay here till the doctors know what's wrong and how to fix it."

Just then her mother walked in, a serious look on her face. "Oh, Lari, you're really awake. I'm so glad, honey." Her mother sounded relieved, despite the worry etched into her face.

"What's wrong with me, Mum? Dante won't say."

Her mother looked at Dante and mouthed a thank you to him. He gave her a wan smile in return. Deb sighed. "The doctors aren't a hundred percent sure... They want to run a few more tests..." Her mother walked to the other side of the bed and took Larissa's other hand. "Sweetie, they said you had a seizure... a couple of seizures, actually. Apparently you had another in the ambulance on the way here."

"Seizures? What? Why?" She looked from her mother to Dante and back again. They both had the same serious, worried expression.

"Oh baby, they think you might have a brain tumour. The doctor wants to run some more tests. They've done some scans and they want to operate tomorrow morning to take a biopsy and find out for certain. They don't have the facilities here, so they're transferring you to Flinders."

"Operate? Tomorrow morning? On my brain?" Suddenly she was terrified. "Dante?"

"I'm here, Lari. Still holding your hand."

"Don't leave me."

"I'm not going anywhere."

"Are they going to shave my head?" she asked her mother.

"Just a small patch. You won't notice it." Her mother looked like she was struggling to not cry.

Larissa was overwhelmed with fear and burst into tears, sobbing uncontrollably. Dante reached over and held her tightly and she clung to him.

TWENTY-EIGHT

She was transferred to Flinders Medical Centre by ambulance about an hour later. Dante and her mother followed the ambulance in his car.

She was given a private room and staff at Flinders let her mother and Dante stay with her all night. Dante pretended to fall asleep, sitting in the chair and laying his head on the bed, still holding her hand. Her mother dozed off in the other chair.

Larissa was too overwrought and terrified to sleep. They were going to operate on her brain at seven o'clock in the morning. As soon as her mother was asleep, Dante gave up the pretence of sleeping.

"You should sleep, Lari."

"I can't. I'm so scared, Dante. I don't want a brain tumour."

"They'll fix it, Lari. They're good doctors."

"Are they going to cut it all out tomorrow?"

He paused, thinking. "No. The scans showed them that they wouldn't be able to do that. You've had this a while, Lari. Those headaches were a symptom." He paused again. "Yesterday morning... I think that was a seizure too... I should've made you go straight to the doctor."

"No. It wouldn't have made any difference, Dante. And it would've ruined my birthday. I had such a beautiful day and you started that."

He smiled sadly. "I love you so much it hurts. I wish there was something I could do to fix you. It's so hard waiting for the doctors."

"Can you be here when I get out of surgery?"

"Yes, of course."

"I want you to be the first thing I see when I wake up."

"I'll be here." Her mother stirred in her chair and he lowered his voice a bit more. "Now go to sleep and rest. I'm staying right here."

"Okay. But kiss me first." She smiled and he smiled back.

"Witch," he grinned at her, kissing her deeply and passionately. "Everything will be okay, my love, and you'll be fine. I promise I'll be here when you come out of surgery."

He put his head down on the bed, keeping hold of her hand. Larissa lay in the bed quietly, her mind racing, trying to process the information that she was going to have brain surgery tomorrow because she had some stupid tumour in her head.

The tiredness was inescapable and despite her worry and desire to stay awake, her eyes closed and next thing she knew she was being woken to get ready for surgery. Dante and her mother were standing by the wall, watching with matching worry on the faces.

"Where's Dad?" Larissa asked, suddenly remembering him.

"Home, with Brad," her mother said. "Well, actually, he's probably about to go to work now," she added, realizing it was six o'clock on a Monday morning.

"Oh."

"He knows you'll be fine, Lari. Don't be scared." Her mother's worried face made Lari think she was lying about her being okay.

"Larissa, we'll both be here when you come out of surgery. The doctors need to do this so they can know how to fix you. Okay? Everything will be fine. You will be fine." Dante's voice sounded solemn and sincere.

The nurses finished what they were doing and left the room. Dante immediately went to her side. "Lari, I love you and you will be okay. Please don't look so scared."

She gave him half a smile. "I love you too. Be here when I wake up, please." He nodded and she looked past him to her mother. "You too, Mum. Be here when I wake up?"

"Of course, sweetie." Her mother gave her one of those wan smiles just as the orderlies arrived to transfer her to a trolley and wheel her away.

"Mum! Dante! Don't leave me!" she panicked.

"We'll go with you as far as they allow," Dante told her and both he and her mother stayed in her line of sight as she was wheeled to theatre.

Finally they came to a set of doors and the orderlies told them it was as far as they were allowed. Her mother kissed her cheek. "I love you, Lari. Everything will be okay and I'll be here when you wake up."

"Dante?" she asked.

"Right here. I promise, I'll be here too. And I love you." He leaned over and kissed her lips gently. "You will be fine," he whispered, staring straight into her eyes. She felt her fear easing.

"I love you," she whispered as the orderlies wheeled her through the doors and away from Dante and her mother.

A few minutes later they transferred her to the operating bed and a nurse inserted a drip in her hand, telling her to count backwards from a hundred.

"One hundred, ninety-nine, ninety-eight, ninety-seven, ninety-six, ninety-five..." her voice faded away on the last number and her eyes closed.

TWENTY-NINE

She opened her eyes. Everything seemed blurry. A nurse was talking to her, asking her if she was awake. "Dante," she said, or thought she said.

"She's not quite with us yet," she heard the nurse saying. "But I think you can take her back to the ward. Her obs are good."

She let the darkness come back. Next time she opened her eyes, she saw Dante's face. Larissa smiled. "Beautiful witch," he whispered, smiling back at her.

"Dante," her voice came out as a croak. "Thirsty," she told him.

He looked at her mother. "Can she have a drink?"

"Oh, I don't know," her mother answered, stepping closer to the bed. "Hey, sweetie. You're back with us. I'll just go ask a nurse if you can have a drink."

"Okay," answered Lari. She reached up to feel her head. It was wrapped in bandages. "Oh," she said, fear edging her voice.

"Looks worse than it is, so don't panic. They drilled a hole in your head to get a piece of the tumour so they only shaved a little patch of hair. The bandage is just wrapped around to protect the surgery site from curious fingers like yours."

She smiled at his explanation. She hadn't even had to ask.

Her mother came back into the room clutching a glass of water with a straw. "The nurse said for you to sip slowly and not drink too much at once," she told her, bringing the glass to her and putting the straw in her mouth. Larissa sipped slowly as she was told. It seemed hard to swallow, almost as if she couldn't remember how.

"Hard to swallow," she whispered, a little less croaky now that she'd had something to drink.

"Temporary side effect," her mother told her. "That's why the nurse told me to tell you to have little sips."

"Oh," Larissa squeezed Dante's hand. "What time is it?"

"Nearly three o'clock. You've been out for hours but the nurses told us it was fine, that they'd checked you in recovery and you'd woken briefly." Her mother brushed her forehead gently. "They've also been in here every hour to take your temperature and check your blood pressure and something else I'm not sure of."

Right on cue, a nurse entered. "Aha, Miss Parker, you're finally with us completely. I've just got to do some obs so bear with me please." She stuck a thermometer into Larissa's ear and then clipped an oxygen monitor to her finger. Next she wrapped a blood pressure cuff around her arm. Noting all the results on the clipboard at the foot of her bed, she removed the clip from her finger and the cuff from her arm. "Everything's fine. I'll be back in an hour. Just press the call button if you need anything."

"Thanks," Larissa told her.

"Lari, do you mind if I leave for a minute and go call your father? He's waiting to hear from me."

"Yeah, it's okay Mum. Thanks for being here when I woke up."

"Not a problem, sweetie and I'll be right back after I talk to your dad." Her mother left to make the phone call, leaving her alone with Dante.

"So, what's the results?"

"They haven't said anything except that the operation was successful. I think they're waiting on results. The doctor told your mother he'd come talk to her about four-thirty."

"Oh, that's another hour and a half."

"Yes."

"Dante, you've been here ever since I got here."

"Yes."

"I know you pretended to sleep for my mother and the doctors and nurses..."

"Yes, I did."

"What about eating and going to the toilet? How..."

"How did I get around that? Toilet was easy. I just told your mother I needed to use the toilet every so often and walked out of the room. Food was a bit harder. I told your mother I was too worried about you to eat and when she insisted, I left after making her promise to stay with you and then I came back half an hour later and told her I'd eaten something."

Larissa smiled. "I wanna go home. When can I go home?"

"I don't know. We'll know at four-thirty, I guess."

"Kiss me while Mum's not here," she asked.

He laughed. "You have a one-track mind." He leaned over and kissed her gently. Larissa wrapped her arms around his neck and pulled him closer, kissing him more passionately. Finally he broke free. "Enough. You should be resting."

"Yes, Lari, listen to your boyfriend," her mother's voice said.

"Mum! When did you walk in?"

"Just a minute ago." Her mother sat in the chair by the wall where she'd slept the night before. "Your father's glad to hear the surgery went well and I've promised to call him after the doctor comes in at four-thirty to tell us what's happening next."

"Can I go home after that, Mum?"

"I'm pretty sure they'll want to keep you tonight at least, Lari. You had surgery this morning on your brain. Possibly tomorrow you can come home." Her mother looked doubtful. "And speaking of home... I should get back there tonight to take care of Brad. Would you mind if I did that, Lari? I'm pretty sure the hospital only let us stay last night because you were having surgery this morning."

"It's okay, Mum. You can go home after we see the doctor. Can I have some more water?"

"Sure." Her mother brought the glass and straw to her lips again and Larissa sipped slowly, finding it slightly easier to swallow.

THIRTY

Right on four-thirty the doctor entered. He was nothing like Larissa imagined. Instead of the balding old guy she'd pictured in her head, a tall blond with tanned skin and blue eyes who looked about forty walked in the room. "Hello. I'm Dr Walker. I'm the doctor in charge of treating you. I didn't actually do the surgery. That was Dr Thomas. He's a surgeon, I'm a specialist."

"Hi," responded Larissa.

"Hello, Dr Walker. I'm Deb Parker, Lari's mother and this is Dante Hill, her boyfriend." Deb pointed at Dante as she spoke.

"Hello, hello," he said to each of them. "Do you want me to talk to just you and your mother or are you happy for your boyfriend to stay?"

"Dante stays." Larissa's tone was adamant.

"Okay." The doctor walked over to the bed. "Mind if I just have a look at you first?" he asked.

Larissa shrugged, her grip on Dante's hand tightening. Dr Walker shone a light into her eyes, her mouth and her ears. Then he unwrapped the bandage, took a look at the wound dressing and rewrapped the bandage.

"Okay, that all looks good." He looked from Larissa to her mother. "There's no easy way to say this so I'll just jump right in. The results are back from the biopsy we did this morning and they aren't very good, I'm sorry to say. She has a glioblastoma. It's not curable by surgery. I've discussed it with my team. We could attempt to remove as much as possible surgically, and then a course of radiation followed by chemotherapy. The goal would be to lengthen her lifespan."

"Glioblastoma? Lengthen her lifespan?" her mother's voice was shaky.

"Yes. Inevitably, a diagnosis of glioblastoma is fatal. There is no cure," he said. "And her tumour appears to be quite advanced. Without further treatment, she probably has two to six months. With treatment we could possibly extend that to two or more years. There are no guarantees, of course. I am really very sorry." He patted Larissa's arm as he finished speaking.

Larissa looked from the doctor to Dante to her mother and back to Dante. Her mother and Dante looked shocked. Horrified, even. Larissa couldn't process the information.

The doctor continued into the silence. "If you're willing, we could schedule her for surgery on Friday and start the radiation a week later. The chemotherapy would begin when the radiation ended. I won't pretend the treatment's pleasant because it's not. She's going to lose her hair, feel very weak and nauseous and probably a lot of other side effects also. Treatment will take at least six months to be completed and then it will probably take another two to three, maybe more, before she starts to feel like she's recovering from the treatment. That's if it all goes well." He paused, reminding them, "Her tumour is rather advanced."

"No! No! No!" Larissa yelled. "I want to go home! Now! Take me home now! Mum! Dante!" Her voice was full of panic and she clutched at Dante's hand.

"Larissa, please relax. We won't make you do anything you don't want to, but really it's not a good idea for you to go home now. Tomorrow. We'd just like to keep an eye on you tonight." The doctor was using his most calming tone.

"When should she start treatment, did you say, Doctor?" asked her mother in a shaky voice.

Before he could answer, Larissa was loudly speaking, "I'm not doing it. You can't make me. I'm not doing it!"

"Look. How about Larissa goes home tomorrow and you take a couple of days to talk through the options. I'll make sure the nurses give you information to take home and read. Let me know what you decide by Wednesday and if you want to go ahead, I'll book her in for surgery on Friday. It's a lot to take in right now."

"I'm not doing it," Larissa muttered.

"Sshhh," Dante whispered.

"Thank you Dr Walker." Her mother's voice sounded shaky.

"I'm very sorry. I wish I could've had better news for you." He started to walk towards the door.

"Doctor! Wait! I have a few questions before you go," Larissa called to him.

"Yes?" he said, stopping and turning to face her.

"If I don't have any treatment, you said I'd die in two to six months."

"Yes. That would be the most likely prognosis."

"How?"

"How?"

"Yes, how would I die?"

"Oh. You might go to sleep one night and not wake up. You might have another seizure and slip into a coma from which you didn't wake or you might have a seizure and rupture something in your brain. There are other variables. You will have more seizures and you may get mood swings, personality changes, headaches, nausea, and other equally unpleasant symptoms. You could quite probably have a stroke or multiple strokes. Read the information the nurses will give you."

"What about if I have the treatment?"

"Well. The same answer applies except if the treatment's successful, it will happen further down the track. If you're one of the lucky ones, it could be two or more years that you survive. Or the treatment itself could kill you. There are side effects to the chemotherapy in particular that can cause death."

"How likely is it that the treatment would be successful and give me at least another year?" she asked him.

Dr Walker paused, looking solemn. "Not very likely, I'm sorry. Your tumour appears to be very advanced."

"Thanks for answering my questions," Larissa told him. "Sounds like whatever I do, I'm not going to make it to twenty-one and probably not even to seventeen."

"No, it's very unlikely. I'm really very sorry." He looked as sorry as he said he was. He turned to face Deb. "Mrs Parker, the nurse will bring you some information. Go home and read it. I'll arrange for Larissa to be discharged tomorrow morning and you can all talk about it at home. Tell me your decision on Wednesday. If you decide against treatment, I'll understand. Again, I'm sorry I don't have better news for you."

"Thank you, doctor," her mother told him, her face still registering nothing but shock. Her mother rushed to Larissa's bedside as the doctor left the room. "Oh baby," she cried, clutching Larissa and holding her tight.

"I don't wanna die, Mum, but I'm not doing that treatment," Larissa sobbed into her mother. "I'm not spending whatever time I have left in hospital."

"We'll talk about it at home. Right now I have to tell your father the news."

"Don't tell him on the phone, Mum. Go home and tell him. Can you ring him and ask him to pick you up? I want Dante to stay with me a little bit longer."

"Sure, baby, I can do that. You don't mind me going home now?"

"No, Mum. Go home and tell Dad. Dante will stay with me until they kick him out. Won't you, Dante?"

"Of course," he answered, his voice husky.

Larissa looked at him, seeing the pain in his face. "You don't have to if you don't want to, Dante," she told him.

"I want to," he answered.

"I'll be okay, Mum, and I'll be home tomorrow."

"I'll bring her home tomorrow, Mrs Parker. As soon as she's discharged."

"Thank you, Dante. I love you, Lari. Think about changing your mind about treatment. Please."

"I'll talk to her," Dante told her mother. She gave him a sad smile.

"See you tomorrow, Lari. I love you," her mother gave her another hug and a kiss and walked out the door.

"She's going to cry," Dante told her.

"I know," Larissa answered. "It's not fair!" Dante wrapped her in his arms as she broke into uncontrollable sobs.

THIRTY-ONE

The doctor arranged her discharge for ten o'clock the next morning and Dante was waiting to take her home from nine-thirty. The nurse put her in a wheelchair and wheeled her to the front entrance. Dante took off to the car park and brought his car around to pull up in front of her.

"Wow. Your boyfriend has a nice car," the nurse told her.

"Yeah, it's pretty cool. So is he," Larissa smiled as she watched him get out and walk over to her. He opened the passenger door and before she could step out of the wheelchair, he'd lifted her and placed her in the seat. "Dante!" she complained. "I can walk, y'know."

"Too late. You're in the car now." He smiled and shut the door. "Thank you," he told the nurse and got back in the driver's seat. "Put your seatbelt on," he told Larissa, seeing she hadn't.

"Why? You won't crash."

"I won't drive till you do."

"Grrrr," she growled at him, fastening her belt. "Happy now?"

"Yes, thank you," he told her as he drove off. "You're very petulant considering you got your own way and escaped from the hospital. I'm pretty sure they wanted to keep you there."

"Yeah, I think they did, too." She stared ahead at the road. "Dante, I'm really not going back there."

"You may not have a choice. You heard what he said. You'll have more seizures."

She shook the brown paper bag in her hand. "Got these to slow that number down." She smiled at him, putting the bag down in her lap and continuing, "Yeah, there's something I thought about last night after you left and I wanted to talk to you about it."

"Talk."

"If you made me a vampire, would I be cured?"

He looked shocked and forgot to look at the road.

"Dante! The road! Watch the road!" she squealed, her eyes wide.

He turned his head back to the road and answered her in a flat voice. "Yes. You'd be cured and you'd be sixteen forever."

"What's wrong with that?"

"In a hundred years you might just be tired of being a sixteen year old girl. You'll never look like a grown woman if you become one of the undead, Lari. You'll look exactly as you do now forever. You'll never have children."

"I'll never be a grown woman if I don't. You heard the doctor. I'll probably be dead before I turn eighteen. Before I'm seventeen, even. And I'm never going to have children anyway. The treatment he wants to give me would make me infertile and besides, you told me we can't make babies together and I'm never leaving you."

"You could live at least another couple of years if you have the treatment he wants and even if you still wanted to do this then, you'd be older... and I'm not getting into any discussion about our inability to reproduce together. Not every woman is unable to have children after chemo, either. Even I know that."

"He also said that it would be unlikely I'd ever get to seventeen, treatment or not, remember? I don't want kids anyway. I'm too young to even think about that."

"You're only sixteen now. One day you might really want children. More than you want to be with me." He looked forlorn.

"I won't. I want you." She frowned. "Okay, say I have the treatment and it doesn't work and I'm not going to get those extra couple of years. He said I'll lose my hair. Even if it does work, I'll lose my hair and it won't grow all the way back before I run out of time. Does that mean if you made me a vampire after the treatment, I'd never have hair again or I'd have baby hair or not much hair, anyway? Or will it come back if I'm made into a vampire?"

Dante looked surprised by the question. "Actually, I think you stay pretty much exactly as you were when it happens. My hair hasn't changed in all these years. Nothing has."

"Have you ever cut your hair?"

"Yes."

"What happened?"

"It grew back to this length within forty-eight hours."

"Mad." Larissa sounded impressed. "So, I want you to make me a vampire and I want you to do it while I have proper hair so I'm not doing the treatment. Besides, I want to spend my time with the people I love, not in hospitals. Maybe it would be different if he said they could cure me, but they can't. Please, Dante."

"I can't. Not right now, anyway. I need to get my head around all this." He paused, contemplating what he said next. "Last night I went home and talked to Kristof and the others about you. I was so upset at the thought of losing you. We talked about the possibility of changing you into a vampire. You understand that if this happened, there are consequences. You'd have to pretend to die in a way that you disappeared. There would be no body for

116

your family to bury. You could never see your family again. It would be too risky. You would have to leave here and preferably go overseas where no-one knew you. I would leave here with you so you wouldn't need to be alone but you would know only me. You would be sixteen forever. You will look this way forever." He paused. "I can't stress this enough, Lari. This is permanent. Forever is such a long time. I've been nineteen for one hundred and twenty years. Every few years I have to move on so people don't realize that I don't age. It can be really lonely. You eat mostly vegetarian and seafood now, but afterwards, your preferred diet will be one hundred percent human blood. And not animal blood. It must be human. We can have other things but vampires need the human blood, we have to have it. Can you cope with that? And there's no guarantee changing you works. You might die and not be reborn anyway." He glanced at her. She was looking at him intently. He turned his face back to the road. "The others are going to leave the decision up to us. Please, Larissa, if you want to do this, I want you to give it more than one night's thought. You can't take it back once it's done. And forever is a very long time."

"I forgot that I'd have to leave my family." She sat quietly, thinking. "Okay, how does this sound? I still want you to make me a vampire but you don't have to do it right away. I'm not doing the treatment and I'm not changing my mind about that. But I want to spend some time with Mum and Dad and even Brad since once I'm changed I can't ever see them again. So, I stay human for now but if the seizures start to get too bad, then you change me. Otherwise, you change me in four weeks before I start to really fall apart."

"Lari, when I said give it more than one night's thought, I meant more than one night and thirty minutes in the car."

"Yeah, but you don't have to do it for ages unless the seizures get crazy. He said they'll get worse gradually and I've got those tablets to take now."

"Okay. Let me think." He said nothing more till they pulled up in front of her house. "I'm not agreeing or disagreeing yet, okay? We need to talk about this some more. I don't want you to just disappear. You need to say goodbye to your family somehow. It still hurts me that my family never knew what happened to me, that I couldn't say goodbye."

"Okay. I love you Dante. You'll be saving my life."

"By killing you."

She threw her arms around him and kissed him. "Saving my life," she whispered. "The tumour is killing me."

THIRTY-TWO

She realized when she got out of the car that despite her assertion at the hospital that she could walk, her walking was actually a long way from good. Dante grabbed her before she could fall and she leaned against him, slowly making her way to the front door. Her mother was waiting for her.

"Lari. Come sit in the living room."

Dante led her to the living room and helped her into one of the chairs.

"Would you like a drink? Something to eat?" her mother asked.

"No, I'm right, Mum. They fed me before I left the hospital and I'm not thirsty yet. Don't hover."

"Sorry, love." She turned to Dante. "Would you like anything, Dante? Thanks for bringing her home and thanks for..." she waved her hand around vaguely, "everything else."

"No, I'm fine, and it was no trouble."

"Sit down." She pointed him to the chair next to Lari and sat in another. She looked at Lari, clearly nervous about what she was going to say. "I told your father when I got home. He was very upset. So am I. We've read the information sheets the nurse gave me. Have you given the thought of treatment more consideration?"

"I'm not doing it, Mum."

"Larissa, you could live another six months to two years."

"The treatment takes nearly six months and is hell. It won't cure me and there's no guarantee it's going to work and give me longer either. You heard the doctor. It's unlikely to give me even one extra year. And it takes nearly as long to recover from the treatment. I don't want to spend the next year like that. If I even last that long. I want to spend whatever time I have left with you and Dad and Dante and even Brad, not in hospital."

"The seizures will get worse."

"They'd probably get worse anyway. And the treatment has other side effects. I'm not losing my hair. I don't want to die ugly and bald. Besides, the hospital sent me home with some tablets I'm supposed to take every day to help make me have less seizures."

"Lari, you're not thinking this through." She turned to Dante. "Dante, can't you reason with her?"

"I've tried, Mrs Parker. Yesterday at the hospital and all the way here this morning. She's adamant."

"Yes, she can be incredibly stubborn. Ever since she was little, she had that stubborn streak." Her mother looked fondly at her. "I don't want to lose my little girl, Lari."

"Mum, it's gonna kill me anyway. Don't make me suffer when I don't have to just so you can stretch out how long I'm on earth. It's not living if you make me do that."

Her mother's eyes filled but she held back the tears. "All right. Your father and I agreed that we wouldn't force you. If the doctor had told us he could cure you, or even if he could've guaranteed us longer with you, there's no way we'd let you refuse the treatment, but because he can't, we decided it's more important for you to be happy. But I'm not happy about this, Lari. Don't think that because you're getting your own way that I agree with you. I don't. I want you to fight to be here and I feel like you're giving up."

"I'm not giving up, Mum. They can't fix me, even if they give me that treatment. I'll fight to stay alive as long as I'm living life, but I'm not doing that treatment."

"Okay," her mother seemed resigned to Lari's decision but she knew her mother well enough to know that the discussion was only over for now and it would start again when her father got home. "I rang your school this morning and told them you wouldn't be in for the rest of this week and we'd work out if you were going back."

"No more school?"

"Lari, it depends on your health. If I have to, we'll home school you. I'd much prefer you went to school but we can't risk you having seizures there. It's far too dangerous. What if you had a seizure on a flight of stairs?"

"Oh." She hadn't given school a thought. She'd made friends and gotten used to the size of the school now and it wasn't as bad as when she first started, but the idea of no school seemed really appealing. "Why do I need home-schooling anyway? Even if I live another couple of years, what do I need school for? I won't have any kind of career."

"It's useful. It fills your time. It makes you smarter." Dante chose this moment to speak.

"Listen to your boyfriend, Lari. He's speaking sense."

"Yeah, right. You only say that coz he's saying stuff you agree with. Why can't I just quit school?"

"No. If you won't do the treatment, I'm putting my foot down about school."

"Ho, ho, ho! That's playing dirty, Mum! Well, fine then. I'll do school coz I'm not doing treatment."

Dante was smiling so she reached across and gave him a light thump. "Ouch!" he said, laughing, even though she knew he hadn't felt any pain at all.

"Mum, can Dante and I go sit in the backyard?"

"Sure. Do you need help walking?"

"I'll help her if she needs it, Mrs Parker."

"Great. Thank you, Dante. You don't have classes today?"

"I'm skipping." He saw Deb's raised eyebrow and quickly added, "Just today. I was too worried about Lari to focus."

"Oh, okay. I understand. Don't skip too often. It's too hard to catch up and you don't want to fall behind."

"I won't, Mrs Parker."

"Okay, I'll leave you to it. I'm going to tidy up around the house. Those boys made a bit of a mess yesterday."

"Okay, Mum," Lari answered her. Dante helped her stand and waited for her to get her balance. "I think my legs are working better now," she told him.

"Yeah, well, lean on me if you need to." He kept hold of her arm and walked slowly with her out into the backyard. They reached the sun lounges and she lay down in the first one, sighing as she took her weight off her legs.

"Wow. That's better. How come my legs feel so wonky?"

"Side effects of the seizure or the surgery. I'm not sure." He dragged the other sun lounge next to her and lay on it. "Lari, you told your mother you'd stay alive as long as you could and yet you know what you ask me to do."

"I said as long as I'm living life. In a month I bet I'll be getting weaker. Look at me now. I can't hardly walk."

"That's temporary."

"Is it?"

"Okay. I don't know if it is or not. Just think about how long forever is, please Lari. Just do that for me."

"I will. But being with you forever sounds really good to me. You do want to be with me forever, don't you?"

"Yes. I can't imagine being without you now. I don't want to be without you."

"Good. Me either. I don't want to be without you. So, I won't change my mind." She saw the look on his face. "I promised to think about it and I will. I'm just telling you that I know I won't change my mind, okay?"

"Okay."

"And one last thing. If my mind goes to mush, does it get fixed when I change?"

"Your physical self is healed during the transition and it would be this disease affecting your mind, so yes, I think your mind would get fixed."

"Good. If my mind goes to mush before you do it, remember that I want this and change me please. Don't let me be a vegetable. Don't let me die like that. Please promise me."

"Oh Lari. You're not going to let this go, are you?"

"No."

"Okay, then. Before I make any promises, I want you to answer one thing for me."

"Anything, Dante."

"If you didn't have... the option of what I can do... would you still refuse treatment?"

"Oh, Dante!" Larissa stared into his face, thinking about her answer. Eventually she replied, "Yes. I would. The treatment won't save my life and the tumour's too far gone for them to even think there's any certainty about giving me longer, so yes, I'd still refuse the treatment. I can't change my prognosis and I don't want to spend however long I have left in hospital getting bombarded with things that make me feel terrible and missing out on time with my family. I meant what I said about wanting to just enjoy the time I have left with the people I love. Maybe I'd think differently if we'd discovered the tumour earlier, but not now. It's just too late."

Dante looked solemnly at her, sitting up and turning to face her fully. He reached across and took both her hands in his, staring deep into her eyes, speaking softly and sincerely, "Then if it's what you really want, I'll do it. I promise you, Lari. Don't rush anything. Take all the time you need with your family and when you're ready, I'll change you."

THIRTY-THREE

A lot of the rest of the week was spent sleeping and crying. Larissa's dad tried to be strong for her but she caught him crying in the back yard the second day she was home. He'd come in from work but hadn't walked inside. Larissa had decided to go out into the yard to watch the sun go down and almost stumbled into him. He didn't see her. He was leaning his head against the shed and banging it with his fists. She could hear him crying. Feeling embarrassed and not wanting him to know she'd seen, she crept back inside quietly.

"Oh, I thought you wanted to watch the sun set, Lari?" her mother asked.

"Ummn... Forgot my camera. I wanted to take a picture," she'd lied. She'd stayed in her room watching out the window till her father came in.

Her legs were working better now. It had taken a day or two for them to improve but she could walk almost normally now. Those first couple of days she'd needed to use walls and people to help her get around without falling. It looked like Dante's assertion that the wonkiness was temporary was right but that didn't mean it wouldn't happen again and maybe next time it would be permanent.

She didn't know if he was going to uni classes or not. She thought he was. Once she'd asked him why he was so diligent about attendance when he didn't need to go. He'd told her that it was because he saw the endless years as an opportunity to study everything that interested him and it helped him blend into society better.

It was Friday night tonight and she'd reminded her parents that they allowed her to go out with Dante until eleven on Friday nights and she intended to do just that. Her mother had argued but Lari wouldn't back down. She told her mother that she hadn't had a seizure all week, although she'd had several headaches and chunks of missing time that she'd tried to hide from her mother. She wasn't sure if she'd succeeded. Dante had known about the headaches but she tried to keep the blackouts from him. He'd come round every day after four and stayed till seven. She missed their drives to Cape Jervois and the dunes at Goolwa but her parents wouldn't let her out.

Larissa studied her wardrobe trying to decide what to wear. She wanted some alone time with Dante tonight and she wanted to get romantic with him. They'd only ever made love once, on her birthday. It seemed much longer than a week ago. She wanted to do it as much as they could before he had to change her. She was sure it would feel different when she was a vampire like him. She wondered if he'd like it better then, if she'd like it better. She loved how he bit her as he got lost in the emotion of the moment and wondered if he'd still bite her when she was a vampire like him and if it would feel the same for her.

The doorbell rang before she was dressed and she realized she'd lost half an hour standing in front of her robe. The doctor had warned her that sometimes seizures would feel like she was missing some time and she worried that she seemed to be having so many of those kinds of seizures, even taking the tablets. Immediately deciding to say nothing in case her plans to go out with Dante were cancelled, she grabbed some jeans and a t-shirt from her wardrobe and pulled them on.

"Larissa!" her mother called. "Dante's here. He's waiting in the family room."

"Coming!" she called back. Quickly she brushed her hair and applied her usual foundation, eyeliner and lip-gloss. She walked out to Dante. "Hey," she said, giving him a kiss. "Where are we going tonight?"

"We're going out?" he asked, glancing across at her mother.

"Yes. We are. And it's Friday night so I don't need to be home till eleven."

"Oh." He glanced at her stony-faced mother and back to her. "Well, as long as you feel up to it."

"Yes, I do." She tugged on his hand. "Let's go."

"Okay. Bye Mrs Parker," he said as he allowed himself to be led out.

"Bye Dante. Bye Lari. Be safe."

"Bye Mum!" called Larissa without breaking stride. "C'mon Dante," she whispered. "Let's get out of here!"

"Jailbreak?" he whispered back, laughing. "Your mother doesn't seem happy about it."

"You don't know what it's like..." she complained as they made it out the front door and into his car. "I thought I'd never see the outside world again!"

"You'll see plenty of it," he smirked. "I thought you wanted to spend this time with your family."

"Yeah, well not all of it. I want some alone time with you too."

"Oh, do you? Does that mean you'd prefer if we drove to Goolwa?"

"Yes. Please."

"Food first?"

"Nope. Just you and me and some alone time."

He laughed. "My one-track Lari is back."

"Are you picking on me?" she asked with a pout.

"No way. I love my one-track Larissa."

"Good."

They drove out to the usual spot at Goolwa, and after parking the car they wandered into the dunes to their usual secluded spot. Dante laid a rug on the ground and they sat down. Immediately, Larissa threw herself at him, kissing him passionately.

Her hands were busy trying to remove his shirt, and unsuccessful, they gave up and snaked back to his hips. "Take your clothes off," she demanded huskily. "And take mine off. I want to be naked with you."

"Larissa..." he whispered.

"Don't argue. Make love to me." She didn't stop kissing him and her hands wouldn't leave him alone.

"Oh Lari..." he groaned and resisted as she kept trying to get his shirt and jeans undone. Without warning, he moved fast and stripped both their clothes from them. The air had a slight chill to it against her skin, but she didn't care. His hands felt along her naked body, sliding up and down her soft skin, cupping her breasts, caressing her buttocks.

"Dante... ohhh, Dante.... Make love to me... please make love to me..."

He kissed her neck, her throat, her breast, slipping inside her at the same time. She felt the same searing sensation as the first time followed by waves of hot pleasure as he sunk his teeth into her breast.

No seizure this time and she felt him drinking, her pleasure escalating. Lari screamed his name, "Dante! Dante! I love you, Dante!" clawing his back with her fingers while her body shuddered in climax.

Afterward she lay entwined with him, panting softly. "I love you," she told him. "I felt you drinking my blood. It feels so... there just aren't any words for how good that feels. Can we do it again?"

He chuckled and shook his head. "No. There's only so much control I have and I don't think it extends to making love with you twice in one night."

"What control do you need?"

"To stop drinking. To remember how breakable you are and not hurt you by accident."

"Oh." She paused, looking at him seriously. "Do you like making love to me? Does it feel good for you?"

"Ohh, you have no idea how good. I love making love with you."

She smiled. "Will it feel better to you when I'm a vampire too? Will it be different?"

"Good question. I don't know the answer to that."

"Have you had vampire girlfriends?"

"No."

"Oh. Why not?"

"I never met anyone I felt that strongly about until you." He paused. "Lari, it took Kristof nearly two hundred years to find Lucinda. It took Cristóbal two hundred and fifty years to find Camille. We found each other quickly. I've only been a vampire for one hundred and twenty years."

"Oh," she smiled. "You make me so happy."

"And you make me happy."

THIRTY-FOUR

"Dante..."

"Yes, my beautiful witch."

"How are we going to do my changing into a vampire?" It was Saturday afternoon, a week after their last visit to the dunes and they were sitting at the beach, off by themselves, watching the surfers. She'd had another seizure the night before when Dante arrived to take her out so there'd been no trip to Goolwa or anywhere else. This time he'd caught her before she crashed to the ground. He'd held her until she came to. She was vague and slurring her words at first but then, just as her mother was about to take her to the hospital, she came round fully and demanded to stay home. Dante promised to stay with her and they watched a movie till she fell asleep. She didn't remember it, but her mother told her he'd carried her to bed before he left for the night.

Today he'd arrived at ten o'clock and promised her mother that he'd bring her straight home if he thought she was tired or had another seizure. She knew her balance wasn't up to riding the board, her legs were wonky again, but she wanted to watch others, so he'd brought her down to the local beach.

He stiffened. "What do you mean? How will I change you? Or how will we arrange your disappearance?"

"The last one first I think."

He looked out to sea. "We've talked about this at home. Camille thinks you should write a suicide note and in it you should tell your family that you're going to swim out to sea until you can't swim anymore. Leave your clothes on the beach. When they don't find your body, they'll think a shark got it. You need to disappear in a way that they aren't surprised to not find a body."

"Dante. That sounds like it could work. But when would I do that?"

"I'll sneak you out at night and we can just pretend you got out yourself."

"It's a good idea. I want to take my surfboard. How can I do that?"

"If you take it with you when you do the fake suicide they'll wonder why they don't find any bits of it."

"Can I leave it at your place?"

"I'd have to give it back. It wouldn't be right not to."

"What if I wrote in my fake suicide note that I wanted you to have it?"

"That might work."

"So, I like Camille's idea. I think it would work and I can write in the note how much I love my 'rents and even Brad. Y'know, a proper goodbye. And

I'll say in it that I want you to have my board." She paused. "You said that I'd need to go away and you'd go with me."

"Yes."

"How will you do that?"

"I'm not going to cope very well with your disappearance and fake death, Lari. I'm going to drop out of uni and return to England as far as your family is concerned."

"Where will we really go?"

"I don't know yet. America, maybe? I haven't been there for many years."

"I've never been out of Australia. Won't I need a passport? How will I get one? I need my 'rents to sign the application coz I'm not eighteen yet."

"Yes, you'll need a passport, but you don't need to worry about that. Kristof is sorting it all out."

"Fake passports? Can you do that stuff?"

"Lari, we've all been vampires for many years and we live among normal humans and have almost normal lives. There are all sorts of things we do to ensure our survival and concealment. There's a lot for you to learn."

"Is Kristof... and the others... are they leaving too?"

"No. There's no need and they're happy here. They'll need to leave in another year or two, maybe a few more, but they'll do it when it suits them."

"What happens to the house when you all leave?"

"Sometimes Kris rents it out I think. I've never asked him. I do know it's not one of the houses he stores his things at."

"Oh. Do you have any houses? And are the ones you store things at different?"

"Yes. I have a house in the countryside near Avebury and a ranch in New Mexico. I store things at the ranch in New Mexico but not at Avebury. And yes, they are different. The ones we store things at tend to be places that disappear easily... ummmnn, I mean people forget that they're around."

"Oh, okay. So, why don't you have a house in Whitby? And will we go to one of your houses?"

"A house in Whitby would be too painful, a reminder of all I lost. Remember it was around forty years before I could bring myself to visit there. Life stretches out so long for me that to me a year feels like what a week does to you." He smiled at her. "We could go to one of my houses or we could go somewhere new. I really haven't thought it all through yet. There's still another two weeks before we do this, Lari. Are you still sure you want to?"

"Yes. But I don't want to wait. I want to do it now. I'm scared. The doctor said that maybe I would go to sleep and just not wake up and if that

127

happened, you wouldn't get to change me coz my heart wouldn't be beating and it needs to be beating, doesn't it?" Her voice got more panicky as she spoke.

"Breathe, Lari. You've had one seizure since you came out of hospital. That's longer between seizures than before you went in."

"Uh no," she interrupted him. "I didn't want to say anything in case Mum went stupid and wouldn't let me out anywhere. I've actually had lots more I think. I keep losing chunks of time and I think I must be having those seizures where I just vague out then or there's no-one around to see it and tell me I had a seizure."

"Oh Larissa." Dante looked crushed. "How often?"

"Every day I lose a chunk of time." The tears welled in her eyes. "I think it's happening faster than we thought it would. I don't think I've got two months, Dante." Her voice choked up. "Every day since I got out of hospital and since the last seizure, it's happened a couple of times a day, even taking those tablets."

He wrapped his arms around her and pulled her close. She sobbed into his chest while he stared out to sea. "Okay. Tomorrow night. You can hide at our place until it's time for us to leave. I'll sneak you out just after midnight, so get your note sorted." He pushed her away from him and stared into her tear-stained eyes. "Are you really sure you want to do this? We can't go back and undo it if you change your mind after."

"I'm sure, Dante. I'm too scared to sleep."

"Leave your window open tonight and I'll sneak in after everyone's gone to bed and stay with you. If you start to slip away in your sleep, I'll change you before it's too late. I promise. But I'm sure you'll be okay."

She smiled sadly at him. "Can you help me write the note?"

"No, it has to sound like you. Write from your heart, Lari. Tell them how much you love them."

"Okay." She was silent for a few moments. "So, how do you change me?"

"Do you really want to know? It's not very pleasant."

"Maybe not. Or not right now, I guess." She leaned against him and looked at the surfers. "Next week I'll be able to surf again. I won't be sick or dying anymore."

"You won't be alive either, Larissa. You'll be immortal but the price is the death of your human life."

"I know, but I'll have you. Forever with you."

THIRTY-FIVE

Dante was as good as his word. She left her window open and shortly after all the lights went out in her house, he slipped silently inside the window. "Oh, Dante," she whispered. "You came."

"I told you I would," he whispered back. "Have you written your note?"

"About a dozen. And screwed them all up. They're in the bin." She waved her hand at the bin beside her desk.

"Good."

She looked at him strangely. "Good?"

"Yes. It makes it look like you spent a while considering it."

"Oh, I guess so."

"They'll go through your things, Larissa. Even the police. Especially the police."

"Oh. I never thought of that."

"You're going to disappear. They won't just let it go. They'll look for you."

"Oh." She frowned. "Help me write the note, Dante. I can't do it by myself."

"You write. I'll listen and make suggestions."

"Okay." She started writing, whispering the words out loud. "Dear Mum and Dad, this is a really hard letter for me to write. I've decided to go out and swim out to sea for the very last time. I want you to know I love you both lots and lots. I love Brad too. I've been having seizures all week, every day, and they're getting worse. I didn't tell you coz I was so scared that you wouldn't let me go out with Dante anymore and I love him too and I wanted to spend every moment I had left with all of you. I'm afraid of turning into a vegetable or something else or going to hospital and dying there. More than anything, I don't want to die in hospital. I've always loved the beach and yesterday when I was down the beach watching the surfers, I realized I wouldn't get to surf anymore. My legs are too wonky to ride my board, or even for me to carry my board to the beach, so I'm walking down to the sea and swimming out as far as I can until I either have another seizure or can't swim anymore. Please don't be too sad. I'm choosing to end my life the way I want, doing something I love. I want you all to remember me like I was too, and not as some invalid in a hospital. I really don't think I have long left, so I'm not really speeding things up by much. Please tell Dante I love him more than anything in the world and give him my surfboard to keep. I want him to have it to remember me. I love you all, Larissa." She was crying softly when she finished. "There. Will that do?"

"Yes." Dante's whisper was hoarse. "Don't change a thing."

She got up from her desk and joined him on the bed, hugging him and sobbing. "I will miss them, Dante. But I know this is the right thing to do and I'm not going to change my mind." She let go of him and sat beside him, leaning her head against his shoulder.

He nodded. "Now give me the letter and all the ones in the bin."

"Why?"

"So no-one discovers them before tomorrow night."

"Oh, yeah. Can you get a plastic bag from the kitchen for me to put them in? I'm scared I'll make too much noise and wake someone. My legs really don't work properly anymore."

"Yeah, I'll get it. Where are they?"

"Second drawer opposite the sink."

He slipped quietly into the kitchen, returning seconds later with a plastic bag. She had the letter ready for him, neatly folded. They tipped the contents of her bin into the bag. He slipped the letter into his back pocket. "Now, go to sleep. I promise you I won't let you fade away in the night."

"Will you be here when I wake up?"

"I'll wake you before I leave, but I'll have to leave before daybreak so no-one sees me."

"Okay." She lay down under the cover. "Will you cuddle me? You can stay on top of the cover if that makes you feel better."

He lay down next to her and she snuggled into him. Less than ten minutes later she was sleeping. He stroked her face gently and kissed her lightly. "Oh my Larissa," he whispered. "I love you so. It breaks my heart to change you but I could never survive without you."

Six hours later as the sun was starting to rise, he gently shook her awake. "Lari, wake up, my beautiful witch." He kissed her lips and nuzzled her neck.

Slowly she stirred. "Dante," she whispered throatily.

"Sshhh. I have to leave now, beautiful."

Her eyes sprung open. "Is it morning already?"

"Nearly dawn."

"Oh." She sat up. "Kiss me before you go. What time will you be here?"

"Lunchtime?"

"Ten."

He raised an eyebrow. "You're not sick of me yet?"

"No." She smiled at him. "Ten."

"Ten it is." He grabbed the plastic bag and disappeared through the window. She got up to watch him leave but he was so fast he'd disappeared before she even reached the window.

THIRTY-SIX

Her last Sunday seemed to take so long. She had another seizure between the dawn when Dante left and ten o'clock when he returned. Luckily for her, it happened in her room and she'd come round before anyone discovered her, so her mother didn't know and she decided not to tell Dante either. She had to concentrate to not slur her words but since she did that more often now, even without extra seizures, it wasn't too noticeable to anyone.

When he arrived at ten, Dante agreed to take her to Goolwa and her mother approved the trip, as long as they agreed to be home early.

They took a slight detour as he wanted to take her for the sightseeing drive through McLaren Vale that they'd never got around to doing before. Eventually they got to the beach around lunchtime. There were windsurfers and sailboats out on the water but their favourite hangout in the dunes was still theirs alone.

Dante had their clothes off in record time and began kissing her. For once, she didn't need to demand it of him. She loved the strong, cold, hardness of his body. This would be their last time lovemaking as vampire boy and human girl. It was as special to her as their first time.

He was inside her without warning and she felt that searing flash that she'd grown accustomed to. He was kissing her throat and licking at her breast but he hadn't bitten her. She surprised herself by how much she wanted him to.

"Bite me," she urged him. "Bite me, Dante." Lari felt the rhythmic fire in her body as he made love to her but she wanted more.

His teeth grazed her skin but he still didn't bite her. Tonight he would change her and part of her wanted him to lose control and do it now. "Please bite me, Dante... I want you to drink from me... please..."

"I can't," he whispered. "I'm afraid I wouldn't stop. I know that I'm going to drink from you tonight without restraint. I can't do it now. I don't trust myself." He groaned and kissed her breast and she cried a little, wanting desperately to be changed now. The heat in her body grew.

She knew it was mean to him but she couldn't let it go. "Please..."

He moaned, "Oh Larissa," and sunk his teeth into her breast, removing them almost immediately.

She buried her face against his chest to muffle her screams of delight. "Dante, Dante, Dante!" she chanted, her body rocking with the orgasm. She clung to him as he held her close, waiting for the orgasm to subside. "Make love to me when you drink from me tonight. Can you do that?"

"No, I can't." His voice was hoarse. "Larissa. I have to get away for a minute." He got up and fled, like the first time they'd been here, so fast he seemed to disappear, only this time he didn't stop where she could see him.

She got up and gathered her clothes, dressing while she waited for him to return. He'd bitten her even though he wasn't sure he could stop because she asked him to. And now he'd fled to regain his control. She understood. Tonight he was making her a vampire like him and she knew how reluctant he was to do it.

He returned before she'd finished dressing, putting his own clothes on at high speed. "I'm sorry."

"It's okay. I understand."

He hugged her. "I'm okay now. I just had to get some space, to get control."

They were home early like her mother asked and Dante pretended to have an assignment to complete so he was gone before dinner.

She spent her last night watching a movie with her family. It was a rarity that they all wanted to watch the same thing, but her mother had borrowed Pirates of the Caribbean 2 – Dead Man's Chest from the DVD store and her brother was eager to see it since he hadn't had a chance to watch it yet. Her parents hadn't seen it yet either. Larissa had already seen it a few times but she'd liked it and would've watched anything if it meant spending these last few hours with her family.

Deb made popcorn in the microwave and they sat and watched the movie in the home theatre her dad had set up for them. It ended all too soon.

"Okay, kids. Bedtime for you both, I think," her dad exclaimed as the credits rolled. "Good movie."

"Dad, can I watch it again tomorrow?" Brad asked.

"Sure kiddo, but only if you get straight into bed now without an argument."

"Okay. Night everyone!"

"Night Brad!" they all chorused.

"Okay, I'm off to bed, too," Larissa told her parents, kissing them both goodnight.

"Night, love. Sweet dreams."

"Night, Lari. Love you," her mother gave her another hug. "Everything all right?"

"Yeah, it's fine. I'm just tired."

"Okay. Goodnight, sweetie."

Larissa went straight to her room and changed into her pyjamas. She crawled in under the quilt and turned off the light. Dante would come for her after everyone was asleep. She waited anxiously in the darkness, listening to the sounds of her parents preparing for bed.

Finally the house grew quiet. Without warning, Dante leapt through the window and landed in her room. She smiled at him and threw off her quilt.

"I'm ready," she whispered.

"Get changed into clothes and take a swimsuit," he whispered back.

She did as he instructed while he emptied the plastic bag of screwed up failed letters into her bin and handed her the folded letter. "Write Mum and Dad on the top of this," he told her, "so they'll know to pick it up and read it."

She scrawled the names and handed him the letter back. He made her bed and placed the letter on top of the cover, standing up on its folds like a little tepee. She left her discarded pyjamas on the floor beside the bed and clutching her favourite black one-piece, smiled nervously at Dante.

"Dante, why won't you make love to me when you change me?"

"Too difficult. I need to concentrate, to be careful... there's just too much involved... I'd be afraid of... hurting you."

"Okay. But can we make out?"

"Yes, we can do that. Now, climb on my back," he whispered. She used the bed for help since her coordination was so poor and got onto his back. Instantly they were away. He moved so silently and fast. They were out the window seconds later. This was like when he carried her to the cave only faster. She closed her eyes and nestled into him, holding on tight. They were at the beach in minutes.

He lowered her to the ground. "Last chance to back out, Larissa. Are you sure?"

"Yes, Dante. Change me."

133

THIRTY-SEVEN

He undressed her so fast she hardly knew what happened, laying her clothes in a pile on the sand. Then he gently lowered her to the ground.

"I love you, Larissa. This part won't hurt, but tomorrow when you change, it will feel like nothing you can imagine."

"I trust you, Dante. Do it."

He gently placed her on the sand, laying down beside her and caressing her naked body. This would be the last time she'd feel soft and warm. He was going to miss her blushes, the softness of her flesh, her warm skin. He kissed her neck, her throat, between her breasts and all the way to her navel. He held her hips and drew himself back up her body, finally finding and kissing her lips, gently at first and growing more passionate as she wrapped her arms around him, pulling him to her. He held his weight off her, rolling them so she was on top.

"Oh Dante, I love you so much!" she cried.

"I love you, Larissa. For eternity, I'm yours," he whispered. "Are you sure you want this? Once I start, I won't be able to stop."

"Do it."

He plunged his teeth into her breast, drinking her blood, sucking harder than he'd ever done before. She groaned in ecstasy, surprized by the pleasure she felt, trying to be quiet. Her body arched and she gripped him with her legs, squeezing her knees against his hips and rocking against him.

"Oh Dante..." she moaned. He placed a hand over her heart and kept sucking her blood. She felt strange, light-headed, as if she was floating away. Her eyes closed and she went limp, collapsing onto him.

Dante stopped drinking and rolling over, gently laid her on the sand. He stared into her pale face, looking so peaceful. He'd drunk so much of her blood that she couldn't survive. Her heartbeat was faint and growing weaker.

"Larissa, my love," he whispered and ripped at the inside of his wrist with his own teeth. The blood flowed from the gash and he quickly thrust his bleeding wrist against her open mouth. Her body reacted instantly as the vampire blood flowed into her.

Her back arched then collapsed to the ground, her hands clawed the air randomly, her legs kicked independently, nothing was co-ordinated. He stayed crouched over her, letting his blood flow into her as her body continued its arrhythmic spasms.

A few minutes later he removed his arm and gave his wrist a quick lick. The gash healed almost instantly and the blood flow stopped.

Larissa lay still and white beneath him. He leaned down to kiss her lips tenderly. Quickly he stood and picked up her swimsuit, tucking it into the waistband of his jeans.

He bowed down and gently scooped her into his arms. Her body was still limp. He tucked her close to his chest and ran to his home at blinding speed. He went over the wall and was greeted at the front door by Kristof.

"This is her?" he asked.

"Yes," answered Dante.

"You've already done it?"

"Yes."

"I thought you would wait till you were here." He shrugged. "Never mind. It was a private thing for you. I understand." He stepped away from the door and signalled Dante to enter. "Come this way. The room is ready for her."

Dante followed him through the large entry to the living room. Camille, Lucinda and Cristóbal were standing around an open trapdoor, waiting. "Oh, you've done it already, Dante." Camille sounded disappointed. "I thought we'd meet her in human form first."

"I'm sorry, Camille. I didn't know you wanted that."

"It was difficult for him, Cami. It was a private thing. You must remember he did not want to change her," Kristof chided her gently. He turned to Dante. "Take her down below and make her comfortable in the room with the lock. Make sure you lock it. Then if you must wait, wait this side of the locked door. Under no circumstances are you to stay in there with her. You understand?"

"Yes. I'll wait down there."

"How long ago did you change her?"

Dante shook his head. "Five, ten minutes."

"You will be waiting at least six hours."

"I'll wait."

"This side of the door, Dante. The locked door. Remember your first awakening. She will be dangerous and thirsty. Do not unlock the door."

"Yes. This side of the locked door and don't unlock it."

"Good. We will prepare for tomorrow. Her people know you live here. There will be visits from police I think. Perhaps even her family. Camille bought food today to make our kitchen look used." He smiled. "We will give it to the needy in a few days, when we don't need it anymore."

Dante smiled, "Only the stuff that hasn't gone off, I hope."

"Ah, yes. We will discard anything that is inedible." He laughed. Kristof reached over and placed a hand on Dante's shoulder. In a more serious tone

135

he continued, "It is not a bad thing you have done, Dante. She would have died and now she will be with you forever and she asked this of you. It was your gift, not a curse."

"She will be sixteen forever, Kristof."

"Better that than rotting in the ground. Remember that when you feel maudlin." He took his hand away. "Now, make us all safe and put her in the room we've prepared for her."

THIRTY-EIGHT

Larissa awoke thirsty. For the first few minutes she didn't even remember who she was. She just wanted blood. She could hear a wild animal screaming and growling, clawing at the walls. She wanted it to shut up and she wanted blood. Lots and lots of blood.

Her eyes suddenly opened and she realized that even in this darkened room, she could see exceptionally clearly. She also realized that the noisy animal was herself.

"Larissa, do you hear me? Lari, it's Dante."

She tilted her head. The noise stopped. His voice was muffled and she looked around the room. It was bare except for the sheepskin rug she'd obviously been laying on. He wasn't here with her.

"Larissa. I know you can hear me. You're thirsty, so thirsty that if I were to go in there now, you'd try to tear me apart. I can't let you do that, my beautiful witch. The door is locked and it will stay locked for now. For your safety and ours, you must stay there a while longer. Your family will know you've gone in about an hour. After that the police will look for you. It will be tonight before I show you the hunt. You need to learn patience and control. You'll start to do that today, in there, alone with your thoughts. I would stay here with you if I could but you know the part I have to play. I have to be the shocked and grieving boyfriend." He paused for a second. "Remember the story I told you about how I was changed and what my creator told me afterward. Remember I told you I couldn't see him? He had locked me away, for both our safety." He grew silent.

Larissa heard the growling noises again, teamed with the clawing. She knew it was her but she didn't know how to control it.

"In a little while, you're going to start feeling things. Your body isn't fully changed yet. I can't describe the way it feels to change, but it's not pleasant, my love. All the changes will be complete by tonight when I release you from here. Camille and Cristóbal and Lucinda and Kristof are all eager to meet you and I love you, Larissa."

"I love you, Dante," she thought, unable to speak yet. "I want you here with me." The animal that was her was throwing itself at the wall between them, hissing and growling and clawing frantically.

"I know," he answered her out loud. "I can hear your thoughts, Lari. When the change is complete, you will be able to hear mine, and your ability to speak will also have returned to you. Don't be afraid." He was silent again

137

for a few moments. The only sound was her furiously scrabbling at the wall, hissing and growling and screaming in frustration and thirst.

"Aha. It seems that your parents discovered you were gone earlier than we expected. Kristof is watching the beach and he's just told me that the police are there and have found your discarded clothes. I must go upstairs now, Lari. I will be back. I promise. We have eternity now."

Dante returned upstairs to the living room. Quickly shutting the trapdoor and covering it with the large floor rug, he made his way into the kitchen. All but Kristof were waiting there, standing like statues, listening to Kristof's thoughts.

He started making brewed coffee. "Start talking like humans. Moving around. I know, we all do it well out in the world but we're not accustomed to pretending to be human in our home. We need to make it so we don't forget and do something out of place. They'll be here after they go back to her parents. Or her parents will. So practice looking human. And Kristof should get off the balcony before he's seen."

"Oh he's thought of that, Dante. He will tell any who ask that he went out to watch the sunrise and saw the police searching the beach and was curious so he forgot about watching the sunrise and looked west over the beach instead. Curiosity is very human, you know," Camille explained.

Dante could hear Larissa screaming in pain, although the noise was beyond the range of human ears. He grimaced.

Lucinda spoke to him gently, "We've all been through this, Dante. She will be all right. She has us. We will all help you. Help her to adjust. Remember, she has an advantage that none of us ever had."

Dante looked at her questioningly, "An advantage?"

"Yes. She asked for the change. She knew she was to be changed. It has got to be so much easier to know before and want it to happen than to just wake up changed, not knowing what happened to you, not asking for it. And she has us to help her through the transition. She has not been abandoned."

"You have a point, Lucy," Dante conceded. "Now, cook some food and throw it out. We need to make this place smell of human things before they come."

THIRTY-NINE

The buzz at the gate came nearly an hour later. Camille was eager to be the one who greeted their expected visitors, so she answered the buzzer. "Yes?" she asked with her thickly accented English.

"This is Steve Parker. I'm looking for Dante Hill."

"Yes. Come in. I will get him." She buzzed the gate open and Steve walked up the path to the front door. Camille was waiting at the open door for him. "He is coming. Can I help you?"

"Ah, no, I don't think so." He looked at the stylish and petite strawberry blonde with pale, creamy skin, barefoot but dressed in skinny denim jeans and an expensive-looking top. "I don't mean to be rude, but you are one of Dante's housemates?"

"Yes. My name is Camille." She smiled at him. "Please come into the living room." She waved him toward the living room, stepping out of the doorway so he could enter. "Would you like coffee?"

"Ah, no thanks," he answered. He stood in front of a luxurious ultra-modern white leather modular sofa, looking at it as if he'd forgotten what to do next. "Do you go to university with Dante?" he asked, his voice slightly jagged.

"Ah no, it is not my... How you say? Thing. My boyfriend Cristo is at uni with Dante and I live here with Cristo."

"Oh." Steve Parker seemed unable to think of what to say or do next. He looked back at the sofa as if wondering what it was for.

Dante appeared in the living room doorway before Camille could say any more. "Hello Mr Parker." Hearing his voice, Steve turned to face Dante.

Dante looked at his face and could see the pain and shock etched there. When he spoke again, his voice had an edge of panic. "Has something happened to Lari? Another seizure? Is she in hospital?"

"Dante..." Steve's face crumpled. "Lari's gone, Dante."

"Gone? What do you mean, gone? Where did she go? It's seven in the morning. And she can't drive."

"She left a suicide note saying she was going to the beach and swimming out until she drowned. The police found her clothes on the sand this morning."

"No!" Dante stumbled backwards into the wall and covered his face with his hands. He found the anguish easy to show when he could hear her screams of pain from below, the sound too faint for human ears but deafening in his own.

139

There was a gasp from Camille. She had her hands over her mouth and a shocked expression on her face. She turned and fled the room, disappearing into the kitchen.

Steve Parker looked broken. "I'm sorry Dante. I know you loved her and she loved you." He sank down into the couch, putting his head in his hands briefly, before looking up again. "She said in the note that she's been hiding seizures from all of us. Apparently she's had them every day since she got home from hospital and they've been getting worse. She was afraid she'd end up back in hospital and that she'd die there and she didn't want that so she chose her own way out." He paused, a faraway look in his eyes. "I don't think it's really sunk in yet. It doesn't seem quite real."

"I'm sorry, Mr Parker." Dante's voice was choked with emotion. "I don't want to believe it."

"I know, Dante. Neither do I. Her mother is a wreck. I don't think she's stopped crying since she read the note. Brad's just shocked. I don't think he's really taken it in yet. I came here to tell you because we felt someone should tell you before you came over this afternoon."

Dante looked sadly at Steve Parker, feeling guilt for the pain of her family, shocked by her sudden and unexpected loss. Listening to her cries from downstairs, he also felt so terrible that he couldn't tell them about her new life but he knew it was impossible to share that information, and that it wouldn't make things right.

Steve continued, "We knew our time with her was running out but we never expected this. Her mother was worried about her last night. She said this morning after we found the note that she knew something was off. Lari watched a movie with us, a movie she'd already seen and she had a sad expression on her face when she kissed us goodnight. She said she was just tired but I think she already knew what she'd planned to do and when she said goodnight she was really telling us goodbye." He put his head back in his hands, rubbing his eyes, before looking up at Dante, his eyes glassy and red-rimmed. "I'm sorry, Dante. You don't need to hear all this. We're all just in shock. I'm going to go now, get back to Deb and Brad. Please stop by this afternoon. If you want to."

"I will. I'm so sorry, Mr Parker. So, so sorry." Dante paused and squeezed his eyes shut. Below, in the basement, Lari was howling in agony. Only the vampires could hear her.

"Me too, Dante. Me too." Steve got up to leave. Dante walked with him to the door. Lari's father hesitated in the doorway, remembering. "In the note she said she wanted you to have her board to remember her by. Make sure you come and get it. Or would you prefer me to drop it off?"

"I... I'll come see you this afternoon, Mr Parker. I can't take it all in right now."

"I understand, Dante." He turned to leave and Dante watched him make his way out the gate.

Larissa wasn't screaming anymore, she was moaning. Dante closed the door and walked to the rug hiding the trapdoor, laying down on it, wishing he could hold her and fix everything but knowing he had to let her endure this. There was no other way.

FORTY

It was just on dusk when Larissa's cries faded into silence. Dante had spent the entire day sprawled over the trapdoor, listening to her alternate between growling and hissing and screaming and crying and moaning.

He tensed, waiting, but the silence lengthened. Then finally, her voice speaking at last, "Dante? Dante? Are you still there?"

"Larissa?" He half-sat, looking at the floor as if he could see through it.

"Oh Dante! I think it's over now. I don't feel that craziness now but I'm still so thirsty." She sounded calmer.

He sighed. "I'm so glad you're through the worst part. And I know how thirsty you are but it's still too early for you to come out. Were you aware that your father came here?"

"No. When was that?"

"Hours ago. This morning. Lari, he looked so sad. I promised him I'd go to your old home this afternoon but I haven't wanted to leave until I knew you were okay."

"I'm sorry he's sad but I was going to die if I didn't change. He would still be sad. You know that." She was silent for a second. "Go to them now, Dante, if I can't be let out yet." She was silent again for few more seconds. "Did he say anything about my board?"

Dante chuckled. "Yes, he did. He told me you wanted me to have it and I was to pick it up or he would bring it here."

"Good."

"Okay, I'm going to go there now. When I come back you can come out and go on your first hunt. I love you, my Larissa."

"I love you too, Dante. Go."

Dante stood and turned to leave, spying Kristof and Lucinda in the doorway of the living room. "Good. She has fully changed now. We will be ready with you to release her in another hour. Not before."

"You don't need to be with me, Kris."

"Yes. We all do." He stressed that last sentence. "She is still dangerous, cunning. She can still be overtaken by the thirst and try to harm you. It is too risky for you to go in alone. We will not let that happen."

"I don't want you to hurt her."

"Neither do we, Dante. But we will protect you and ourselves. We cannot have a savage wild vampire running loose here in this community. You must understand this. We talked about it before you changed her. You could not hurt her. You would let her tear you to pieces and still not hurt her. We all agree on that. So, we must all be there. It is how it will be."

Dante sighed. He spoke to Larissa through the floor, "Do you hear them, Lari? I know you won't hurt me. But they will be with me when I return, to protect us all. Be sure you have control of your urges by then, my love." He looked at Kristof and Lucinda. "Okay? I accept your conditions. This is your house. Now I must go play the grieving boyfriend for her family."

He drove his car to her parents' house although he almost decided to walk. It was only when he remembered that he would have to collect her board that he decided to take the car. He didn't want Steve Parker to feel obligated to drive him back home because of the board. It wasn't fair to his housemates to have their sanctuary invaded by humans unaware of their true nature because of his actions.

Their house was the only place they didn't have to pretend to be something they weren't. The others were understanding of the potential for human interaction in their home because of the way in which Larissa had become a vampire, and Camille had done very well this morning, but he didn't want to encourage the Parkers and make them feel they could just drop in, particularly since Larissa was actually in hiding there. She, too, needed to be freed from her basement prison.

He pulled up in front of the Parkers' house. Brad was sitting on the front porch, playing with his PSP. He looked up when he heard Dante's car door close. "Dante!" He stood up. "Lari's not here anymore. She killed herself at the beach," he told him, sadly and quietly.

"Yeah, Brad. Your dad came to see me this morning and told me then. Sucks, hey?"

"Yeah, it does. She was my sister and y'know, she was a pain but sometimes she could be cool. And I loved her too."

"Yeah. She was pretty sick, though. You knew that didn't you?"

"Not really. Well kinda. I knew she was sick coz she went to hospital and then she didn't have to go back to school and then y'know, Mum and Dad let her pretty much see you anytime she wanted, but they only told me today that she was going to die soon, even if she hadn't... y'know..."

"Yeah." Dante stood quietly, looking at Lari's brother who was struggling to make sense of everything. "She loved you, Brad. And your mum and dad. I think she didn't want you guys to see her suffer and not be able to do anything about it coz they couldn't fix what was wrong with her."

"A tumour in her head."

143

"Yeah. The doctors told her it could change her personality, make her mean to you guys, before it killed her. I think she didn't want that to happen either."

"Yeah? I get that." Brad leaned back against the wall. "I miss her, but."

"Me too. Skipped uni and did nothing all day, just thinking about her."

"They didn't find her body. The cops said they probably won't."

"Oh." Dante waited for him to say something else, but when Brad stayed quiet, staring out to space, he continued, "Well, I better get inside to see your parents. I told your dad I would."

"Okay." Brad waited, "Dante?"

"Yeah?"

"Is it okay for guys to cry?"

"Yeah. Especially when someone they love dies."

"Okay. Thanks Dante."

Dante looked apprehensive as he walked in the door. He wasn't looking forward to this. Her brother was so hurt and stunned, Dante was sure her parents would be worse. He felt like a criminal, knowing she was in his basement, immortal now, and he was letting them think she'd died forever last night in the sea.

FORTY-ONE

Dante arrived home a couple of hours later. He removed her board from his car and stored it in the alcove with all their boards and sporting goods.

The others were all waiting for him by the trapdoor. Kristof spoke, "She must be very thirsty by now, Dante, and I think it is safe for her to come out. But you will run with her some distance from here to feed. Yes?"

"Yes."

"Good. Let's do this."

Kristof lifted the trapdoor and waited while Lucinda, Camille, Cristóbal and Dante leaped below before leaping down to join them. Once in the basement, he went to a cupboard and removed some weapons; a sword, daggers, two spears and an axe. He took the sword for himself and offered the remaining selection to everyone else.

Camille took the two daggers, Lucinda reached for a spear and Cristóbal took the axe. Kristof offered the remaining spear to Dante. "I'm not taking that in there."

"Dante," Kristof began.

"We both know I won't use it so it's pointless. Put it away or give it to someone else."

Kristof knew there was no point to argument so he returned the last spear to the cupboard. "Are we all ready?" They all nodded. "Then, it is time. Be on your guard, everyone."

Dante moved to the locked door, the others in a guard behind him. "Larissa?" he asked.

"Dante? I'm in control, Dante. Really thirsty but in control."

"Good. We're opening the door now. Don't move. Where are you standing?"

"I'm on the rug you left here. Do you want me to move somewhere else?"

"No. Stay there and don't move when we come in. Okay?"

"Yes."

Dante turned the key in the lock. Gently he pushed the door open. Larissa was standing on the rug, not moving. He smiled at her. "Good girl. Don't move yet."

"I won't. I'm very thirsty, Dante. It's making it hard to think."

"I know. Not long now and you can drink." He stepped all the way into the room, making space for the others to follow him.

Larissa gasped. "Oh, they're all so beautiful."

"So are you, Lari. Wait till you see yourself." Dante walked all the way over to her, slowly and carefully, the others keeping pace behind him, fanning out as they entered the room. Larissa remained perfectly still.

"When can I move, Dante?"

"Soon." He stood next to her. "You're doing really well. Now, I want you to give me your hand. If they think you're going to hurt me, they'll hurt you so please don't do anything to make them think that, okay?"

"Okay." She held out her hand to him and he took it.

"Now you're going to walk slowly with me out of this room. Don't do anything except walk and hold my hand. Please."

"Okay. Where are we going?"

"Somewhere you can hunt and drink."

"Oh, good. I want to behave for you but I don't think I could do it much longer without a drink. I'm so very thirsty."

"You're doing great, Lari. Tomorrow this will all seem like a bad dream. After your first drink you'll feel so much better and you won't ever go too long without blood again."

"Okay. If it's okay with you Dante, I think I won't talk anymore for a little while. I want to concentrate on doing what you tell me."

"Okay, beautiful." He looked at her as they reached the trapdoor. "You really are incredibly beautiful."

She smiled at him and looked up at the opening. "Do we go up there? There's no stairs or ladder."

"Yes, we have to go up there. Kristof is going to leap up first, then I will, and then you. The others will follow after. Then I'll take you where you can drink."

"Okay." She let go of his hand. Kristof leapt up into the living room, followed quickly by Dante. "Dante?" she asked.

"Just think of yourself up here and leap. You'll do it easily."

She leapt and not knowing what was above the opening, stumbled, landing awkwardly near Dante. "Oh! That felt wicked. Can I run fast now, too?"

"Yes." He smiled at her joy. "Wait for the others, then we'll go."

The remaining three vampires leapt up from the basement, landing gracefully.

"I wish I could land like that."

"You will. Once you know your strengths." He looked at Kristof, who nodded. "You pass, Lari. Time for us to run and hunt. Take my hand." He held out his hand and she grabbed hold. Instantly he began running, so fast they were a blur, up the stairs and off toward the big open deck. He didn't slow down as they reached the balustrade; instead he leaped over it, taking her with him.

She gasped in delight, in awe at how far they flew through the sky before they landed. Her eyes lit with pleasure, she smiled at him as they ran through the night. Twenty minutes later they were miles away and he slowed to a standstill.

FORTY-TWO

"Welcome to Moana Beach, Lari. Far enough away from home for tonight." They stood at the edge of the road, looking down over the sand. The beach was quiet and dark. "Do you see that man asleep over there?" He pointed at a shape at the other end of the beach.

Larissa was stunned to realize she could see him clearly. She could hear his heartbeat. The thirst rose up in her and she growled softly.

"Lari..." Dante's voice was soft but firm. "You need to listen very carefully so you learn how to drink without killing him or being discovered. Are you listening?"

She blinked twice, and then slowly turned to face Dante. "I'm listening, Dante. Tell me what to do."

"You need to get some mind control over him before you can drink from him."

"How?"

"It comes naturally, like drinking. Stare into his eyes, concentrate, and tell him he's dreaming of you. Bite him and drink. Keep a count and don't drink for longer than sixty heartbeats at a time or you won't be able to stop and he will die. If you drink too deep, he will die. Tell him he will forget this dream." Dante looked at her. "Are you ready?"

"I think so."

"Go." He watched her run fast and silently to the sleeping man. She lay next to him and stroked his face till his eyes opened. Staring into his eyes, she began softly chanting the mantra that he was dreaming and that he would forget this dream in the morning. Then she bit into his neck. The blood flowed into her and she was blown away by the way it made her feel. Remembering to count, she stopped at forty, unsure how much she'd drunk before she started counting.

Wanting more but knowing she had to stop, she reminded him that he would not remember her and told him to go back to sleep. To her surprise, he obeyed. She watched his neck with the same fascination she had for her own breast when she was human and Dante bit her. The fang marks faded completely in only a few minutes.

Dante appeared beside her. "Larissa?"

"I stopped. Will he live?"

"Yes." He smiled at her. "I think you're a natural at this, my beautiful witch. I will hunt with you tonight but I have no need to drink. Run with me." They ran inland, with Dante finding a couple camping on someone's field.

Larissa knew what to expect this time and when the blood flowed into her, she was prepared. She started counting as soon as the blood started flowing. Finally, the thirst had vanished. "Oh Dante, that bloodlust has gone."

"Good. You'll drink a few times almost every day for the first month and then it will settle down to two or three times a week. If you drink regularly, it won't return, but if you try to go without for too long, it will come back. That's when you're likely to do something stupid so don't ever let the bloodlust take over. Remember to drink regularly, carefully."

They ran back towards his home on Witton Bluff. She stopped at the Onkaparinga dunes. "Dante," she said softly, knowing he could hear her.

He stopped and looked at her. "Yes?"

"Do you want to... I want you to... "

"Yes, Lari." He smiled at her confused expression. "I can hear your thoughts. Can't you hear mine?"

She tilted her head while she concentrated on listening telepathically. "Oh, yes, I can!" Larissa smiled and leaped over to him, hugging him. "Oooh Dante! Can I still blush?"

"No." He grinned.

"Good, coz if I could I would be!" She laughed softly. "Stop thinking those things and do them!"

He kissed her passionately, falling to the ground with her. His clothes were off in seconds. Her own hands moved just as fast stripping herself naked. He kissed her neck, her breast, her belly. She sighed with anticipation, her hands brushing against his smooth, marble-like skin. Dimly, a part of her brain registered that he didn't feel cold anymore.

He seemed more confident, less hesitant and Lari realized it was because he wasn't afraid of hurting her anymore. For the first time, he was on top of her, no longer afraid of crushing her. The sensations were magnified and Larissa was moaning with pleasure. Every touch felt more intense and passionate and her desire grew stronger. Deep in the throes of passion he bit her and drank while her body arched in orgasm as she cried out, "Dante! I love you! I love you! I love you!" Her own teeth sunk into him in response and she was overwhelmed by the pleasure she got drinking from him.

He pulled away from her, his hands still holding her tight, "Larissa," he said in a throaty voice.

"Do it again, Dante," she told him, rolling on top of him and kissing his lips. "This feels so good!"

He smiled and obeyed.

"Can we do it again?" she asked as soon as they were done.

"One-track Larissa," he laughed. "Yes. For the rest of the night if you wish."

"I wish," she told him, licking at his ear. "This is even better than I could ever imagine. Thank you for changing me, Dante."

He looked into her eyes, startled. "You're really happy?"

"Oh yes. Happier than I've ever been." She looked at him mischievously. "Now, make love to me again. I want more!"

He laughed and complied.

They made love for what seemed like hours, exploring each other's bodies as if they'd never experienced them before, drinking from each other in turn.

Finally, they rested. "Oh!" she gasped. "I just realized... Dante, it used to feel like fire when you made love to me, good fire, but now that searing kinda burn didn't happen."

"Because we're the same now, my love."

"Oh." She smiled at him. "I liked it then but I like it even more now."

FORTY-THREE

They arrived back at Dante's home before dawn. Larissa was amazed at how great she felt. Once she'd drunk, the raging thirst that had dominated her from the time she'd awoken as a vampire had gone and she'd begun to fully appreciate all the things she could now do. And making love with Dante as a vampire like him was the most amazing thing she'd ever experienced.

She realized exactly how fast Dante could run, and that it was much faster than she'd ever imagined, and now she could run just as fast. They could leap so far it felt like flying and she loved it. She knew now why he'd been so afraid of breaking her when she'd been human. Her new strength was beyond her imagination. She could see so far and so clearly, even in the dark. She could hear people's voices from almost a kilometre and their thoughts from within a couple of hundred metres. There were so many people in that range that it was cacophony and Dante had spent part of the night teaching her how to control what she heard so she could shut some of them out. He also explained how to shield her thoughts from other vampires. So many of the questions she'd had for him that hadn't been answered weren't mysteries to her anymore. Now she had new questions.

So much had changed for her in the last twenty-four hours, she hadn't had time to fully appreciate not being able to see her family anymore or the impact her disappearance would have on them, but she knew there'd come a time when it would. She knew their voices and thoughts had been part of that cacophony and she was relieved there'd been too much noise for her to single anyone out. She wasn't sure she was ready to hear their pain. She believed Dante when he told her she'd suffer not just losing them but also feel their pain at losing her. But there was a stubbornly practical streak in her that knew her loss was unavoidable to them, no matter how it ended up happening and she hoped that would make it easier for her when all that emotion finally hit.

All Dante's vampire housemates were standing in the living room waiting for them when they returned. Again she was stunned by how beautiful they looked. She knew that even with human eyes, she would've thought they were incredibly attractive, but her new vampire eyes saw them as exquisitely perfect.

They were all pale-skinned. There was a dark-haired and honey-eyed man of average height and solid build who had seemed to be in charge earlier when they were downstairs. Larissa imagined him to be Kristof.

"Yes, I am Kristof. This is my house. Welcome." He had an indefinable accent, a deep voice and an almost old-fashioned way of talking.

"Thank you," she answered, surprised they were speaking. "Do you always talk when you could just share your thoughts?"

"It is a habit we maintain so that we don't forget when in human company."

"Ahh." She looked at the others. Next to Kristof was a petite and curvaceous beauty with pale green eyes and long copper coloured hair that fell to her waist.

"Lucinda," she told Larissa with a smile and a southern American accent.

Next to her was another petite and beautiful slender girl with strawberry blonde hair styled into a shoulder-length bob. She looked straight at Larissa with caramel eyes. "Camille," she said in heavily accented English.

Lastly, standing next to her was a tall and slender, deceptively muscular man with denim coloured eyes and shoulder-length dark brown hair. "Cristóbal. " he told her in a heavily accented voice.

"Oh, your voice is like my mother's favourite actor!" She thought for a second, "Antonio Banderas!" she exclaimed.

Dante laughed, "Perhaps because Antonio and Cristóbal are both from Spain."

"Oh, are you?" she asked him. Before he could answer, she continued, "Nice to meet you all at last," smiling as she spoke, feeling as nervous as if she was meeting Dante's family for the first time.

"You also, Larissa. You have captivated Dante, something no other girl has done in the many years we've known him." Camille smiled back at her. She tilted her head to look at Lari more speculatively. "You are thinking we are all very beautiful." She smiled and continued, "More beautiful than you. But you have not seen yourself yet. I think you should be shown a mirror." In a blur, she was standing next to Lari and guiding her to the huge mirror on one wall.

Larissa saw a petite and pale-skinned beautiful girl with pale violet eyes and golden blonde waist length curls staring back at her from the mirror. "Oh wow! I look like you all!" She whirled to face Dante. "Dante! It's... I look... oh!" she was lost for words and flung herself at him, hugging and kissing him. "I'm so, so happy! Thank you, thank you, thank you!"

She released him and returned to the mirror, staring a few minutes longer, turning to study all the vampires in the room with the same degree of thoughtfulness. "Y'know, I don't really look sixteen anymore. I mean, we all look young, but somehow..." she thought for a minute, looking at each of them in turn. "Ageless. We all look young and ageless."

Dante raised his eyebrows, contemplating the idea as he looked at each of the vampires in turn. Finally he answered, "I've never thought of it like that, but I think you're right. Perhaps because I know all our ages, I just see us as frozen in time, but yes, ageless. I think it's true."

FORTY-FOUR

"And now that the introductions are over, we must talk business." Kristof smiled but his tone was serious. "It would be unwise for you to stay here. Of course, you may stay for the rest of the week. It will take me that long to organize the paperwork you will both need. Travel and identification documents. But you must stay hidden and hunt miles from here so that you are not discovered and even then, you must be so careful since there is no body for your family to grieve over, any sighting of you could cause a search to begin. Please, do not stand on our balconies or decks, even at night."

"Oh," Larissa listened to him, nodding her head. "Yes, I understand."

"You understand that you are welcome to join us again in the future when we have relocated? That we do welcome you and it is merely that it is unsafe for you to stay here that makes it urgent for you to leave?"

"Oh, yes, I really do understand," Larissa tried to reassure him that she knew why he wanted them to leave.

"Have you decided where you will go?"

Dante answered, shaking his head, "No. Not yet." He looked at Lari. "We could discuss that today?"

"I've never been overseas, so anywhere would be fine with me," Larissa told him.

"One other thing..." Kristof paused and looked at them both. "The passport..." he frowned slightly. "I thought it would be best to make Larissa eighteen for her passport. And her name... We should give her a different last name. It's possibly silly. They won't be looking for an eighteen year old with her name, but... I'm just cautious."

"Hill," Larissa spoke, turning quickly to look at Dante. "If that's okay with you?"

He smiled. "You'd like my name?"

She shrugged with a half-smile, glad she couldn't blush anymore. "Yeah. Can I?"

"Yes." He looked pleased. Then he smiled at her mischievously. "Of course, if you're going to use my name and we're travelling together, we're going to have to tell people we're husband and wife or they'll think it strange when we carry on as we do."

Larissa giggled. "Oh my, made into a vampire and married in just a couple of days!"

"We're not really married," he grinned at her.

"Close enough for me," she nudged him. "Hey! I can thump you properly now! No more weakling human thumping a rock!"

"Oh no," he laughed. "I'm done for."

"Then it's settled," Kristof interrupted their play. "I will organise a passport for Larissa, British to match yours but she will be listed as Australian birth. Her accent is too clearly Australian. She will take your last name. It will be done before the end of the week. I will also get your travel documents to America. Is there any place in particular, Dante?"

"Fly us into LA and organize a car for me." He paused and thought. "A new Dodge Viper. Tinted windows, of course. We'll drive to my ranch in New Mexico first and work out where we go from there. Tell me how much you need and I'll transfer the funds."

Kristof nodded at Dante. "After it's done." He turned his head to look at Lari, "One last thing, Larissa."

"Yes?"

"I need a photo for your passport. We can do that sometime today?"

"Of course."

"Then it's all arranged. Decide from where you wish to travel and we will arrange your departure. I suggest you drive to Sydney or Melbourne and fly out of there. You don't want to take any chance that someone thinks they recognize her and you are flagged as travelling with her."

"Melbourne, then," Dante told him. "Larissa is from Sydney. You don't know anyone in Melbourne, do you?"

"No," she answered.

"Good. It's settled. I'll organize everything and you can both leave by Friday." He looked directly at Larissa. "You must be very careful to not be seen, for all our sakes."

"I will. Thank you, Kristof."

He ducked his head. "It is nothing. I am glad that Dante has finally found someone. Eternity is much more bearable with someone to share it with." He left the room and Larissa realized that the others had also gone, leaving her alone with Dante.

"So, Friday we go. I'm excited, Dante. Show me the world." She grabbed his hands and twirled him round.

Dante smiled and stopped their spinning, pulling her close and embracing her. "You are so amazing Lari. It doesn't bother you, your family?"

"Yeah, a little, but I just keep telling myself that they were gonna lose me anyway and it doesn't seem to feel all that real yet. And I've shut out all the random voices in my head so I don't accidentally hear them. It'll be better when we're away from here and I don't have to do that or hide."

He nodded. "I love you. For eternity my immortal witch."

She smiled. "And I love you forever, my immortal lover."

THE END